# GIVE ME FOREVER

THE BEAUMONT SERIES - NEXT GENERATION

GIVE ME FOREVER
THE BEAUMONT SERIES:
THE NEXT GENERATION
HEIDI MCLAUGHLIN
© 2022

COVER DESIGN: OkayCreations.
EDITING: Edits by Amy
PROOFING: YR Editor
PHOTOGRAPHY: Regina Wamba
MODELS: Jade & Talmage

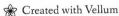 Created with Vellum

*For Taylor Swift*
*Your songs help me tap into my emotional side.*
*I appreciate you!*

# THE BEAUMONT SERIES

## THE BEAUMONT SERIES READING ORDER

Prequels:

Forever Mason

Finding My Way

🐾

Forever My Girl

My Everything

My Unexpected Forever

Finding My Forever

12 Days of Forever

My Kind of Forever

Forever Our Boys

Holding Onto Forever

My Unexpected Love

Chasing My Forever

Peyton & Noah

Fighting For Our Forever

A Beaumont Family Christmas

Fourth Down

Give Me Forever

1

## BEN

The other day at work I overheard my co-worker talking about his girlfriend. He said she was fun and always up for a good time, and it got me thinking about how I would describe Elle to someone if they asked. The first thing I would say is she's my best friend, followed by the love of my life, and then I would add how she's strong-willed, determined, loves fiercely and with her whole heart, and her family is the most important aspect of her life, aside from music. I would tell my co-worker about how beautiful she is, and how I can spend hours watching her long, chestnut hair blowing in the wind. I would tell him how I feel when she walks into the room, even when I'm in the middle of drafting an advertising plan or she's had a rough day and just wants to sit with me.

I'm listening to Elle talk instead of focusing on my current project. She's on the phone with her mom or sister by the tone of her voice. When it's business, she's matter of fact. It's her way or the highway—something I've learned by working for her management company over the years. In her line of business, she needs to be direct. Other managers have tried to show she can't hack it in the industry, only for her to prove them wrong. Sinful Distraction is well on their way to stardom, and she's in the process of signing two new bands. To say I'm proud of her is an understatement. Elle's doing exactly what she set out to do—changing the music management industry.

I look outside at the graying sky and wonder if there's a storm coming or if December is going to be a dreary month in Malibu. I think it's been a week since I've seen the sun, although the lack thereof hasn't deterred any of the surfers. Every morning when I go for a run, they're out there, welcoming the early morning waves and the quiet solitude before the traffic starts and tourists arrive. I close my laptop and make my way outside to get the mail. While most of our bills are online, all our packages come to the house. I'm elated to find a catalog full of wedding invitations and internally fist pump because this means we're one step closer to finally nailing down a wedding date. We've already decided to get married in Napa at one of the vineyards or in Tiburon overlooking the bay, and just need to pick a date.

Elle comes out of the office and finds me in the living room flipping through the catalog. I've dogeared a couple designs I like and plan to show her. She sits down next to me, leans over, and kisses me on the cheek before righting herself. "What are you looking at?"

I close the magazine so she can see the front. "Came in the mail today. It's a sign for us to set a date and finally get the ball rolling."

"That was my mom on the phone," she says, changing the subject. "Aunt Josie has rented a house in Stowe, Vermont, for Christmas and we're all going. It'll be fun, although I'm not sure about the snow. It's cold there, but whatever. We need to go buy some snow suits. We can rent skis there if we want to or just hang out at the house. There's a hot tub as well so we definitely need to bring our suits. I'm not sure what we are going to do about the presents though. I guess we can pack them in a suitcase."

I glance at Elle. She's focused on our Christmas tree and the pile of presents underneath. "I think it would be a pretty awesome present for your parents if we tell them a date."

"For what?"

"For our wedding." I hold the magazine up and shake it. "There are some cute invitations in here. We could make one online and put it in a box for your parents."

"We don't even know if the venue is available. People literally book it out a year in advance, if not more."

"Maybe we need another venue," I say, shrugging. "Or go to the courthouse. I'm tired of dragging our feet."

"I'm not," Elle replies.

"You're not what?" I ask.

"Dragging my feet."

"I didn't say you, I said we. We own a house together. We love each other. We want to start a family. We are financially stable." She is, and I am because of her. "I don't understand what we are waiting for. I already told you I'd sign a prenup if that's the hang up."

Elle stands, ignoring everything I just said. "Where are you going?"

"To the sports store. We leave tomorrow."

"Can you please sit down and discuss this with me?" I wait for a minute or two and when she doesn't return, I go to our bedroom. I lean against the door jamb and watch her before asking, "Why do you keep brushing this aside?"

Elle sighs. "I'm not brushing anything aside, Ben. I'm saying, let's discuss this later, like after the first of the year.

Right now, we need to go to the store and get some clothes to wear otherwise we're going to freeze to death there." She passes by me. When she gets to the end of the hall, she says, "Are you coming with me to the store?"

"No and the store can wait. It's not going anywhere. Hell, I'm sure you can call, and they'll send the entire store to you if you run out of time." My steps are loud as I walk toward her. She backs up until we're in our living room.

"I hate when you say things like that. You make it seem like I'm some spoiled brat."

"Not my intention, Elle. But this is important to me. I'm tired of waiting for us to start our lives. I want to get married and start a family."

"And we will."

"When?"

"I don't know, Ben. When I'm not busy," she says. "When I'm not in the middle of trying to launch a tour for Plum and finalize a record deal for Talking Til Dawn. You know how hard I worked on getting these bands, I need to put my best foot forward and get their careers started."

"I want our wedding to be a priority to you, Elle. Right now, it's so far down your list, you make it seem like you don't want to get married."

"I do, Ben. I love you more than anything, but our lives are busy, and I really feel like you're picking a fight for no good reason."

I scoff at her words and shake my head. "Our wedding day is a *good* reason. Starting our lives together is a *good* reason. But if we have to wait for you not to be busy with work, then we'll be waiting forever because you get busier by the day. Right now, my life is nothing but waiting for you. I wait for you to tell me where we are going and what we're doing. I'm waiting for *you* to sit down with me and set a date, which is funny, because the date doesn't even matter as long as it fits into your schedule. I'm tired of waiting, Elle."

"Where is all of this coming from, Ben?"

I groan loudly and push my hands through my hair, rubbing the tension that's suddenly appeared at the back of my neck. "Why can't you see this from my perspective, huh? Why can't you see I want a family with you? That I want to be your husband?"

"I do, Ben. And I want those things too, but not enough to cause World War III between us. I don't understand how earlier things were fine, *we* were fine. One minute we're talking about the trip to Vermont and the next we're fighting all because this stupid magazine shows up." Elle picks the catalog up from the table and throws it across the room.

"No, I was talking about getting the ball rolling on our wedding." My head shakes back and forth. I draw in a breath and release it before continuing. "No, you told me we're going to Vermont. You didn't ask if I wanted to go."

"Why would I ask, Ben? You've literally spent every holiday with my family since we were in high school. Why would I assume you wouldn't go on this trip?"

Elle leaves and heads into the kitchen. She opens cupboards and drawers and then slams them shut before storming back into the room. "Know what I don't get? Where all of this is coming from. Things are fine with us, we're happy. We're living a great life, why do you want to change everything?"

"I don't want to be like your parents," I tell her.

Her mouth drops open. "You don't want to be happy? What kind of nonsense is that?"

I sigh and look at her. "You know what I mean."

"I'm not sure that I do. I feel like I'm beating a dead

horse here because I don't understand where all of this is coming from. Last week our biggest issue was whether you're buying a gas or electric Range Rover, and now all of a sudden, it's setting a date. Honestly, I'm confused. We agreed to a long engagement until our careers were where we wanted them to be. You've switched your career path from working for someone, to going freelance, to going back to corporate. That doesn't seem settled to me. And now, you're fighting with me about setting a date that may or may not work for the venue we agreed upon. More so, one that you chose. So, help me out here, Ben. Is there something else going on?"

I shake my head. "I've changed my mind."

"About us?" Elle's voice cracks.

"No, about a long engagement. I'm entitled to change my mind, right?"

"Why are you so hostile right now?"

"Because I don't feel heard, Elle." My voice raises in frustration. "This is something I want, and it shouldn't even be something that has to be discussed until we're blue in the face. My wants should be important to you."

"They are," she says quietly.

"Peyton and Noah didn't have a long engagement," I point out.

Elle scoffs. "Peyton and Noah knew they were getting married when they were kids. They're hardly an example to use."

"And I've known I wanted to marry you since high school. I get that it took you a bit longer to figure it out, but you did and now here we are. Why don't we go to the courthouse in the morning and get married?"

"That's an unfair request."

"Why?" I counter.

"Because I want my family there. I want my dad to walk me down the aisle. I want my sister to stand next to me. Jesus, Ben! Do you even hear yourself right now?" She stands there for a moment, rubs her temples, and then turns to leave.

"Where are you going?"

"To the store. I think we need some space before we say something stupid. I'll FaceTime you when I'm there and you can pick out the jacket you want."

"I'm not going," I tell her.

"Clearly, since I just said we need some space."

"No, Elle," I pause and wait for her to come into view. "I'm not going on this trip."

"What?"

"You heard me."

"What do you expect me to tell my family?"

I shrug, not caring. "Tell them I moved out."

"Over a fucking wedding date! Are you serious right now? I'll set the damn date after the first of the year, why does it have to be today? You know full well we'll have to change it because you have to check with the venue first. Jesus Christ, Ben. What in the hell is going on?"

"I'm just done." My shoulders sag when my brain registers what I've said. I don't quit. I don't give up, but this time I am. Right now, it feels like the weight of the world rests on my chest, and there isn't anything I can do about it, except quit. Quit everything.

"You're done?"

I nod. "I think I am."

"Wow," she says. "Just like that?"

I shrug, my voice flat and without emotion in my reply. "I'll be out by the time you get back."

Elle shakes her head. "Don't bother."

2

--------

ELLE

*B*en's phone rings in my ear. I've lost count of the number of rings that sound out before his voicemail picks up. His voice is gone, and in its place is a generic computerized one telling whoever calls that it hopes they have a great day, and their call will be returned shortly. I hang up and press the green button to connect my call again. In the other room, my family chatters about Noah's football team and how they're doing really well. And just like every year prior, there's hope that the Pioneers will go to the Superbowl. This time, I leave a message telling Ben when my plane will land. Peyton and Noah fly back before anyone else, and Quinn and Nola are heading to her parents until after New Year's. Jimmy, Jenna, and Eden are heading to Hawaii to finish off Eden's winter break. The Westburys and my parents are flying to Beaumont for the rest of the holiday. There are a lot of people who want to meet baby Oliver.

I lean against the window and stare into the dark sky. It's a clear night, and I can see the stars—a rarity in California. Ben would love it here. I don't think he'll ever understand

8

*how missed he was at Christmas. I have a pile of presents to bring home to him. Most of them are from my mom. She loves him like he's her son. And he missed meeting Oliver. I can't wait to introduce Ben to the baby. He's going to love him. I look down at my phone and wipe a fallen tear. Ben will never understand how hurt I am that he decided not to come. I can't even remember the last time he wasn't at a holiday or family function.*

*There's a knock on the door, and then it opens. I glance at my mom, carrying Oliver in her arms. "He's sleeping," she whispers as she lies him down in his playpen. She comes over to me and pulls me into her arms. "What's wrong?"*

*I shrug and let out a small sob. "Ben missed so much on this trip."*

*"I know. But we can celebrate Christmas when we get back home. It doesn't have to be on the day itself. Besides, I'm sure his mom loved having him home."*

*I hate lying to my family. "I hope she treated him well." I already know she didn't. She rarely sends him anything, and he's always the one who has to reach out to her. I swear, it's like she can't be bothered.*

*My mom stays for a few more minutes before heading back to the other room. I make my way over to Oliver and sit in the chair next to his bed. This little boy has no idea how lucky he is. It's not because my parents can provide for him, it's because they are the best parents in the world. They have so much love to give. I'm honestly surprised it's taken them this long to add to our family. I'm sure with raising Quinn, Peyton, and I, they probably thought they were done, but here they are, taking on a baby when Peyton is trying to make them grandparents.*

*Oliver fusses, and I wonder if I should pick him up to*

*console him. I know next to nothing about babies, yet the urge to hold him, snuggle him against my chest, is strong. I relent and scoop him into my arms until he's nestled in the crook of my neck. His tiny baby breaths tickle, but I welcome them.*

*He still and lets out a small, contented sigh. When I met him a few days ago, he was just a tiny baby, and now he's my brother. Even if my parents don't end up adopting him, he's going to know he was loved when he was part of our family.*

*I adjust him to rest in my arms. This gives me a chance to stare at this face. His eyelashes are long, perfect. His cheeks have the slightest hint of red; they're chubby and pinchable, and I realize I'll hurt anyone who tries to hurt him.*

*My finger traces a line down his nose and over his lips. He puckers and then stretches. I know I'm breaking every parental sin out there by touching a sleeping baby, but I can't help it. Oliver's eyes flutter open, and we stare at each other. I expect him to fuss or let out a scream, but he doesn't. He looks at me, blinking every few seconds. Does he know I'm his big sister? It's unlikely, but maybe he sees me as security.*

*"Hi, cutie." I pull out my phone, turn on the camera, and adjust Oliver so we can take a selfie. I send it to Ben with the caption:* Oliver says, Hi, Uncle Ben! *I wait for Ben to respond, but he doesn't.*

*"I don't know what I'm supposed to do, Oliver."*

*He stretches and yawns. I frown, knowing I woke him from his slumber. I stand and hold him to my chest. We walk around the room, and I sing to him until he's asleep. Instead of putting him back in his crib, I lie him on the bed and fall asleep next to him.*

"Do you have any kids?"

I clear my thoughts and smile at the lady next to me. She told me at the beginning of our flight that her daughter is eight months old, teething, and not enjoying the flight to LAX. The woman is apologetic and on the verge of tears each time her baby fusses or cries.

"No," I tell her. "My parents are fostering a baby though. He's just a couple of months old."

"I love my daughter, but—"

"She's not bothering me," I tell the mother. "She's a cutie." I touch the little girl on her nose, and she tries to bite me. I laugh, but the woman is horrified.

"She puts everything in her mouth. She likes to test those chompers."

"I can imagine."

The intercom crackles and the pilot announces our descent into Los Angeles. I'm excited to be home, see Ben, and fix the issues we were having before I left. Every part of me hoped Ben would've shown up at the cabin, and things would be back to normal, but he didn't, despite my many texts.

I inhale deeply and try to calm my nerves. Ben hasn't responded to a single text of mine since the night of our fight. I don't know whether to expect to see him at baggage claim or find him idling along the curb. He's never left me stranded before, and I can't imagine he would this time.

After the plane lands, I help the mom next to me gather her things and then follow her off the aircraft. I wish her well when she has to stop and wait for her daughter's stroller and thank the universe she's not a Page Six subscriber and recognized me as Harrison James' daughter. I meander through the airport with just my ballcap on. It's late, and there aren't a lot of people waiting around. I let

Ben know I've landed, and don't bother to wait for his reply. Anxiousness and dread wash over me even though I fight to stay positive. *He'll be outside*, my mind repeatedly says as I make my way to luggage claims.

I don't know how long I stand outside, up against one of the pillars, waiting for Ben to arrive. The minutes tick by, and then a full hour. LAX is quiet. There's a lull in arrivals due to the early morning hours. With each set of headlights that appears, my heart races at the thought of Ben driving toward me, but each car passes by.

"Can I call someone for you?" The porter approaches cautiously. "Do you need a taxi?"

I start to shake my head but then nod. "That would be great, thank you."

He radios for someone to come to the terminal, and within minutes a yellow car pulls up. I climb into the backseat, shut the door, and fight a wave of tears.

"Where to?"

"Um . . ." I should give him my address, but I don't. I give him the address to the studio. I have a couch in my office, and I'll sleep there for the night. The fifteen-mile drive usually takes over an hour unless it's three in the morning, and then it's twenty minutes. I hand the driver a wad of cash and wish him a happy New Year before climbing out. He pulls away the second I slam the door, leaving me standing on the sidewalk. It's cold, but nothing compared to what we experienced in Vermont. I look at the sky, wondering if Los Angeles will ever see snow, and then laugh at my thoughts. The entire city would shut down in straight panic if it snowed.

Thankfully, I have the keys to the studio and make my way inside and to my office. I collapse on the couch and let the anguish I feel rush freely. My sobs turn into hiccups, and any make-up I have on runs down my face. I don't bother changing and lie on my couch with my knees pulled to my chest. I don't know how to fix this issue with Ben, especially if I can't get him to talk to me.

When I wake, it's because of the sounds I hear in the other room. My assistant, Debra, walks in, startles at the sight of me, and then quickly closes my door. "What are you doing? Are you okay?" she whispers.

I sit up and rub my face. She hands me a box of tissues and then goes to my refrigerator and pulls out a bottle of water. "Thanks."

"What happened?"

I shake my head. "Ben and I fought before I left for the cabin, and he hasn't returned any of my calls or texts."

"Oh, Elle."

I sigh heavily. "I don't know how I'll face him this morning. I want to jump into his arms and strangle him at the same time. This meeting is going to drag on forever."

"You need to get cleaned up." She stands and starts rummaging through my bag, setting the things she needs on top of my desk. Thankfully, I keep a steamer in one of my desk drawers, and she gets to work on one of my shirts. "It's a good thing you don't work for someone because you look like shit."

"It's a good thing I like you, or I'd fire you for saying I look like shit." I stand and head into the tiny bathroom attached to my office. Someday, I'll be in a high rise with an ensuite and a view that looks over the city. Until then, I'm happy with what I have. The rented space is perfect for my bands and me.

Debra laughs, knowing I'd never let her go. She runs this place, and I know it. She appears in the doorway with my shirt and leather jacket. "You need to feel like a badass this morning."

"But I don't feel that way at all."

"I know, but this morning, you need to. The meeting won't take long. Plum are already here, all three women."

"Plum," I grimace. "I'm still not sure I like that name for a band."

"It's catchy," she says. "It's one word, and people will remember it. Plus, it fits the personality of the girls. It screams pop with an edge."

Usually, I'd talk to Ben about it and get his take because he is the one who will do all their marketing. "I'll ask Ben when he gets here; see what he thinks."

Debra nods and tells me breakfast will be on the table. After she leaves, I finish cleaning my face and reapply my make-up. I take my hair and pull it into a high ponytail. It's messy and yet perfect for this business.

When I enter the small conference room, the lead singer of Plum stands up. "Good morning, Justine, Wynonna, and Priscilla." They echo my sentiment and sit down at the table. I first met Justine Floyd at Trixie's. Quinn and I had gone to check out a new band, and Justine put on an acoustic set. That night, we spoke, and she told me she usually performs with sisters Wynonna and Priscilla but that they had the flu, and they didn't want to lose their gig at Trixie's. I brought them into the studio and fell in love with their sound, and I quickly offered to represent them. They have quite the backstory. Justine ran away from home at fourteen and somehow managed to escape the horrors of living on the streets. Wynonna and Priscilla, aptly named after Wynonna Judd and Priscilla Presley, are upper class and privileged. The three of them met at Trixie's during an open mic night and decided to play together.

We start the meeting even though Ben's late. It'll be easy for him to catch up, plus he needs to show the girls their mock-ups. After an hour, I text him and ask him if he's planning to show up, and of course, he doesn't respond. Now, I've gone from hurt to pissed because he's messing with my business. I tell the girls the logos will be emailed, and I'll see them tomorrow for recording. Once they're gone, I ask Debra to cancel the rest of my day and order an Uber to drive me out to Malibu.

I'm on edge the entire drive, and my anxiety increases tenfold when the driver pulls into my driveway. When I get into the house, I notice the amount of trash piled up. "What the fuck," I mutter before yelling Ben's name and storming through the house.

I find him in his office with his headphones on. I tap him on the shoulder, scaring the crap out of him. He glares at me.

"What are you doing?"

"Working. What does it look like?"

"Did you want to answer any of my texts? My calls? Or show up for the fucking meeting this morning?"

He frowns and rolls his eyes. He goes to put his headphones back on, but I yank them away. "*Answer me!*" I scream.

Ben stands and towers over me. His eyes seek something in mine, but I have no idea what he's looking for. "What part of 'I'm done' wasn't clear to you?"

"Excuse me?"

"I'm done, Elle. That means I'm not going to answer your calls. I'm not going to reply to your texts, and I'm not going to work. I. Am. Done!"

I blanch at his words and step back. It takes me a moment to realize the finality in his voice, but once I do, I nod. "Right." I leave him in his office and head into our bedroom. It's a mess. Clothes, food boxes, and beer bottles cover the floor, much like the rest of the house. I pull as much as I can from my closet, carry it out to my car, and pack up the stuff I'll need in my office. I stop by the room where Ben's working, but his back is to me. He's angry, all because we haven't set a wedding date.

"Ben," I say his name loud enough for him to hear. He stops typing and turns slowly in his chair. His eyes are red and puffy, and there's a sadness there, mixed with anger. "I'm going to head back into the city." I swallow the lump in my throat. "There's a good chance Noah's heading to the Superbowl."

"I don't care," he says.

"It's Noah," I point out. "You're not going to be there for him?"

Ben hangs his head. "Don't make this harder than it already is, Elle."

"I'm not doing anything, Ben. You are. I spent my entire vacation trying to get you to talk to me so we can figure this out, and you've ignored me."

"It's the only way."

"No, it's not," I tell him. "We can fix this."

"There's nothing to fix."

"So that's it, huh? You're just going to toss the only family you have aside because I haven't settled on a wedding date?"

Ben doesn't say anything for a long time. "I'm going to look for an apartment or something. I'll be out of here as soon as I can."

I shake my head and place my hand over my stomach to curb the tremendous ache I feel. Our life together isn't supposed to be this way. I pack as much as I can, and tiptoe back to Ben's office. His head is down and the urge to go to him is great. I yearn to touch him, to soothe him, to fix what is happening, but I don't know how. There is something else going on, something more than not setting a date, but he won't talk to me. He leaves me no choice but to walk away for now.

# 3

# ELLE

6 Weeks Later

The fanfare at the stadium is something I've never seen before. People tailgate. They're throwing parties in the parking lot, with food, music, and games. Some have televisions set up and they're watching the pregame. Each time I hear Noah's name, I block out what the announcer says. I don't care to hear whether or not they think the Pioneers should be in the Super Bowl or not. They're here, and that is the only thing that matters. Win or lose, Noah's dreams of making it to the big game have finally come true.

Nola and I walk around the parking lot, taking in the energetic atmosphere. I've been to concerts where the tailgating is a giant party, but not to this extent. Venues normally open the parking lot two, maybe three hours before a concert starts, unless it's a festival. Still, I'd love to see 4225 West or Sinful Distraction have something like this.

"I'm hungry," Nola says. My stomach growls loud

enough for her to hear. She covers her mouth and cackles. I roll my eyes and pray no one else heard it.

"Thanks." It's her fault. Lately, food doesn't interest me. My mother has picked up on the fact I've lost weight and barely eat. I don't have the heart to tell her or anyone in my family about Ben and what we're going through. How do I tell my loved ones when I don't understand myself?

"We can head into the stadium and get something," I tell her.

"Or we can introduce you to people, tell them who you are, and see what they give us." Nola waggle's her eyebrows and she smiles like the Cheshire cat. Nola doesn't care that she's intermingled with a famous family, and rarely tells people who she's engaged to, until she wants something. Even then, she's joking. She's never used Quinn's name to get anything from anyone. She likes to tease though.

"Or we go find my dad and drag him around the parking lot with us."

Nola's mouth drops open and she gasps. "Oh my, can you even imagine? We wouldn't make it past the first row. Of course, if we did this, I'd have to get a bullhorn to let everyone know Harrison James walks among us."

This time, I laugh. More times than not, my dad and uncles can mingle without anyone realizing who they are, until it's too late. Of course, there are those super fans who recognize them immediately and alert everyone else to their presence.

"I can't believe we aren't sitting in a suite today. Do you think anyone is going to bug Quinn?"

I shake my head. "They haven't yet," I point out. "He's never in a suite when he's in Portland, neither is Liam. They like to be where the action is."

"Yeah, true." Nola sighs. "Truth be told, I don't want to wait in line for food."

I laugh at her statement. There are definite perks that come with being who we are or who we are related to. "Tell Peyton, I'm sure she can set something up."

"You tell her," Nola says as she bumps her shoulder with mine. "If it comes from you, it won't seem like I'm looking for handouts."

"Peyton would never think that of you," I tell her. "You're going to be our sister, we love you."

Nola beams and throws her arms around me. We hug it out for a minute in the middle of the parking lot, with tens of thousands of people surrounding us, and no one knowing who we are. It's an amazing feeling. I suppose if my hair wasn't tucked under a ballcap and I had on my Noah Westbury jersey, someone might give us a double take. As is it, everyone is either wearing a Pioneers jersey or one for the other team. It's nice to blend in.

We make our way to the family entrance and show our passes. Nola grabs my arm and drags me to the family area where there's food. I lean in and ask in a hushed tone, "Are you pregnant?"

Nola stops dead in her tracks, turns, and looks at me. Her eyes are wide, scared. "Why would you ask such a thing?" she asks in a noticeably clear southern accent. Most of the time, I barely hear it because I'm used to it, and she works hard to speak without a drawl. I actually don't mind it and think it's rather cute. It gives her character, and she stands out among the rest of us, which isn't a bad thing.

"You're yanking my arm out of the socket for a hotdog."

"Not just any hotdog, Elle. *The* hotdog. Ballpark hotdogs are the best."

"We're not in a ballpark," I point out. "We're in a stadium. What if the hotdog sucks?"

She waves her hand and dismisses me. "Same diff."

I'm not sure it is, but who am I to argue. "You didn't answer my question."

Nola starts to walk, but I stand there. She turns and puts her hands on her hips and juts out her right leg. "I am not pregnant."

I shrug. "Wouldn't matter if you were."

"It would to my parents. Those southern values run deep. My mother harps on me every time we talk about how Quinn and I are living in sin, and how we should be married by now. How no one likes a long engagement. Lord, I could go on and on."

I close the gap between us and place my hands on her shoulders. For a brief moment I'm about to tell her about Ben, and how he feels the same way, but then I stop, and start to wonder if there's something wrong with us—Quinn and me—because we're both engaged but haven't set wedding dates. Unlike Peyton, who couldn't walk down the aisle fast enough. I chalk her quickness up to her accident and the fact that she knew she would marry Noah when she was five.

"It's a new era," I tell Nola. "We're allowed to have long engagements."

"Are we though?"

*I honestly don't know.*

After Nola and I stuff ourselves on hotdogs, which I have to admit are pretty damn good, we make our way to our seats. The stands are filling fast now that the opening musical act has finished their melody of hits. As a manager, it troubles me that people opt to forgo opening acts. The artists playing deserve and have earned their time on stage, and it leaves an empty feeling in their stomachs when they look out to the crowd, knowing it's a sold out showing, and hardly anyone is sitting. You'll never see it on their faces because they're grateful for the opportunity to play, but as a manager, it's irritating.

Nola goes to sit, while I head to the front row and nestle myself between my grandparents. I put my arms around them and pull them to me. Neither protest as I squish them into my sides. When I release them, my grandmother looks at me with a sad smile.

"Why are you sad, Elle?"

*How does she know?* It's a stupid question, really, because grandmas know everything. "I'm just tired." It's not a lie. Living in a hotel room sucks. I miss my house, my bed, and my Ben. "I've been really busy at work. I have two new bands, plus Sinful Distraction is going on tour soon."

Grandma smiles, but it doesn't reach her eyes. She brushes my hair behind my ear and her fingers rest on my neck for a moment.

"Are you sure?"

I nod. "I promise. It's exhausting building a business."

"You need a partner," Grandpa says loudly. "Tess and I worry about you kids all the time, overextending yourselves. Hire some help."

"Yes, sir." I don't argue with him because there's no point. Plus, he's not wrong. I have one assistant, who could probably use an assistant. It's bad enough I have to replace Ben. In the six weeks we've been apart, I've gone through two marketing companies and neither of the people they've sent over can deliver the way Ben could.

When I hear my mother behind me, I kiss my grandparents on their cheeks and tell them to enjoy the game. It's not that I don't want to sit with them, I do, but I want to hold

Oliver and if my grandmother gets him first, I won't stand a chance.

I linger on the steps for a minute because my mom has handed my baby brother to Julius Cunningham's girl-friend. She bounces Oliver on her legs and makes the same faces I do at him. My mom had a custom jersey made for Oliver, with Westbury on the back. It's the cutest thing I've ever seen, aside from Oliver. I can't take it anymore and head to the aisle where he is and hold my hands out for him. Autumn hands him over and I go sit down.

"I've missed you," I tell him. I rest my feet on the seat in front of me and set Oliver on my legs. He's wearing shorts and a pair of baby Nikes which match his jersey. "Look at you, being the cutest boy here."

Oliver coos in response and lets out a small giggle.

I play with his legs, touch his cheek, and love on him until I feel a tap on my shoulder. I look at Oliver and shake my head. "No, we don't care who's behind us, do we?"

He smiles. Another tap.

"Who is it, Oliver? Can you tell me?"

When the person behind me clears their throat, I know it's my sister.

"Oh phooey," I say to the baby. "Do you want to see that other sister of yours or stay with your favorite."

"We're both his favorite," Peyton says. "Now hand him over."

I bring him to me and kiss his fat cheeks before handing him to Peyton. I think about joining my mom, but decide to stay where I am. I turn in my seat and touch Oliver's leg. "Is Noah ready?"

Peyton shrugs. "It's a big stage. The biggest of his life. He's as ready as he's going to be."

"It's too bad you can't sit with us," Nola says as she leans into my sister and touches Oliver's cheek.

Peyton smiles and makes some baby noises at Oliver, which earns her a soft coo. "I'm right where I want to be."

"How's Uncle Liam? Did you see him before you came out?" I ask my sister.

"No, he and Dad are in the dressing room."

"Uncle Jimmy is pissed he's not here," I add. "Mom said Eden has some huge event in Australia tomorrow, and they had to fly there early to kill the jet lag."

"Liam said they're going to livestream the game. Although, it won't be the same. The atmosphere..." Peyton pauses and looks around. "This is incredible."

I tap Peyton on her knee. "You've earned this too." I pick up on bits and pieces of Nola's conversation with Autumn. The poor woman is thoroughly confused by our family dynamic. It's comical, in a way, but I get it. Peyton likes Autumn, and so do I.

Nola tells Autumn about her chart, and how she had to write everyone down in a journal so she could keep us all straight.

"Yeah, Peyton tried explaining it to me. I just nodded along," Autumn says as she leans over to look at my sister, who shakes her head.

"I love telling people my sister married my aunt and uncle's son—that really gets people going." I can't help but laugh at my joke. "Their faces are priceless."

Peyton slaps my shoulder and I pretend it hurts. "You're a brat. Where's Ben?"

"He had to work. He's got a big project." It's the same lie I've told for the past six weeks.

"A project that couldn't wait until Monday?"

I shrug, signaling the end of that conversation. Peyton

hands Oliver back to me and tells us she will see us later. As soon as she's on the field with her headset on, everything in the stadium shifts.

It's time for football.

We stand for the anthem, which my uncle nails. Everyone cheers for him, and some chant his name when he finishes. Noah is there to give his dad a hug, which brings a new wave of emotions from me. I pull my phone out and text Ben: Did you see Noah and Liam hug?

He's not going to respond. He hasn't since I left for Christmas. Blue bubble after blue bubble with no response, yet I still text him.

Text after text.

**We won the coin toss.**

**Touchdown**

**Oh my gosh, so cute! Julius gave his son the football from his touchdown.**

**OMG we are tied. I can't take it**

**I'm not sure Aunt Josie is going to make it through this game in one piece.**

**Ouch, did you see that hit on Noah?**

**I really wish you were here. Everyone misses you.**

**Did you know Eden has a surfing event in Aussie tomorrow . . . or is it tonight? I wonder if it'll be on ESPN or something.**

**I think when Liam retires, he's going to take up coaching. He yells at Noah – A LOT!!**

**Bianca has a dirty mouth. I swear the officials can hear everything she says. One looked**

**over his shoulder and I think she shrugged at him.**

**Touchdown!**

**We're going to win this game. I wish you were here to see this. Are you at least watching it on TV?**

**We won, Ben. Noah is a Super Bowl champion.**

I put my phone away and celebrate with my family. Noah makes his way to my sister and picks her up. He twirls her around and when he sets her down, he kisses her long and hard. A pang of jealousy hits me. Their love affair is one of a kind; destined to be together from the moment they met. At times, I feel like Ben and I have the same kind relationship, but in reality, I'm alone and no longer with the love of my life. I glance down at my engagement ring and wonder when I'm going to take it off.

Noah and Peyton make their way to the stands. Our parents and grandparents are there to meet them. When my sister makes her way toward me, I start to cry. This moment, and many others, almost didn't happen. I pull her into my arms and squeeze tightly.

"I'm so damn proud of you, P."

"We did it. We fucking did it!"

My sister isn't one to cuss, so for her to drop the f-bomb, I know she's excited. She's worked hard to prove herself in the league. A league filled with men. This victory is more than just a win, it's putting women front and center of a male dominated profession.

# 4

# BEN

*a*fter the housekeeper leaves, I sit down on the couch and look around. The tile floors shine, and sunlight shines through the windows making parts of it sparkle. The coffee table gleams and reflects my silhouette. She left the windows open, and the sheer curtains blow in the breeze. The voices of people outside unloading their car are audible. Without looking out the window I know traffic is bad by the sounds of horns honking. It's a gorgeous day and people are outside, likely skipping work and school. At another time in my life, Elle and I would've been doing the same, either sitting on the beach or at her parents' house where there is more privacy. Instead, I'm sitting here, in a house too big for one person—and honestly two—hating how clean it is. When there is clutter and trash everywhere, the house doesn't echo. Now, if I talk to myself or walk down the hall, I feel like someone answers or follows me. I'm growing a strong hatred for this house, but I can't leave. I don't want to.

*Because she's still here, even though she left.*

I'm happy she's gone—until I start to think about her.

Once the thoughts roll into my mind, depression takes over. I'm glad my new employer allows us to work from home. If I hadn't taken this job months ago, I'd be face-to-face with Elle right now, in some meeting. It's nice that most of my work is remote and I can meet with clients via teleconference if needed. I don't know what I would do if I had to see someone in person. Right now, I live in my sweats, and put on a sport coat or a nice shirt when I have a meeting. My slacks and jeans don't fit—I've lost too much weight. I should go shopping, but Instacart and DoorDash won't deliver from Macy's and Nordstroms, and I'm afraid to use Elle's personal shopper. The last thing I need or want is a bill or for Elle to call or show up. Her texting me all the time is hard enough.

I think about responding and asking her stop, to say more harsh words to her so she'll get the picture. I don't want to hear from her. I don't want to know about her work, what's going on in her life, or how Noah won the Superbowl. I watched it . . . by myself. It would've been nice to have people over, but I don't have any friends. I have Quinn, but he was at the game. I guess I *had* Quinn. I'm sure Elle has told him to steer clear of me. Any friends I had from the first company I worked for, went by the wayside when I started working for Elle. Since I've known her, I've kept everyone at bay out of respect for her family. I guess I should've known better because now I have no one. Ending things with Elle has opened my eyes to just how much of my life was dictated by her family. The sad part is, she wasn't doing it, I was. I thought I needed to be a hermit to protect her.

Now, I enjoy it. I like not having to shower every day or worry about people stopping by. I appreciate being able to walk outside without people staring, wondering where they've seen us before. When I'm on the beach, people avoid me. They give me a wide berth. I think it's because my hair is shaggy, and the beard I'm growing looks rather scraggly. I don't like myself much right now, but I also don't have the energy to change things.

I turn on the television and lie down on the couch. With the guide pulled up, I scroll until I find something interesting. Deep down, I know I should turn the TV off. I don't pay for any of the apps on there. Hell, my "half" of the expenses don't even come close to what gets paid by Elle for us to live here . . . well for me to live here. My name may be on the deed, but I can't afford this place. She can. She pays for the lifestyle I'm used to. Yet, here I am, mooching off her because she would never kick me out. What does that say about me? Not much. I've ridden her coattails for as long as I can remember, and the one time I tried to break away, I went right back to her because I've been in love with her most of my life. I'm still in love with her but we can't be together. If we can't see eye-to-eye on something as simple as setting a date for our wedding, then how can we survive the marriage? I don't see how we could.

My phone vibrates. I ignore it. It starts moving across the table indicating someone's calling. Still, I don't look. It's my day off and there isn't anyone I need to talk to, let alone *want* to talk to. It's probably Elle. Although she prefers to text; she does call occasionally. I know I can't continue to avoid her, but I'm also not ready to sit down and hash all the details out. I should probably start looking for another place to live. It's either that or move back to Beaumont where it's more affordable because Malibu is so far out of my price range, it's laughable.

The doorbell chimes and I groan. I'm intent on acting like I'm not home, but when Quinn's voice shouts my name,

I know I don't have a choice. With a herculean effort, I get up from the couch and make my way to the front door.

"You look like hell." Quinn steps into the doorway, forcing me to move. He has takeout and the smell of chicken lo-mien makes my stomach roll. The food is from my favorite place, but the thought of eating doesn't appeal to me.

"Thanks. It's good to see you too. Why don't you come in." Quinn doesn't hear me because he's already in the kitchen pulling plates out of the cabinet. I stand there for a moment, looking out the door. I fully expect Elle to come around the corner, but she doesn't. I don't know if I'm relieved or saddened by the fact she's not here with Quinn. After another minute, I finally close the door and make my way toward the kitchen, only to find Quinn sitting on the couch. If his sister were here, she'd yell at him for having his feet on the coffee table and eating food while sitting on her leather couch. But she's not here, so I don't say anything.

"Aren't you going to eat?" Quinn asks without taking his eyes off the television or his food. I can't really tell.

"Yeah." I don't get up because I lack the energy to care. Quinn turns and looks at me for a moment. "Go eat." It takes me a couple of seconds before I heave myself off the couch and make my way into the kitchen. He brought all my favorites, but none of it looks appetizing. Still, I take what I'd normally eat and grab a fork. I hesitate before going back into the living room, still expecting Elle to bust through the door any second and start yelling at us for eating there.

"Missed you at the game," Quinn says when I sit down.

"Yeah, sorry. Some friends showed up unexpectedly."

Quinn removes his feet from the table and sets his plate

down. He doesn't look at me and keeps his focus on the television. "Thought you had to work?"

*Shit*. So, Elle told her family I had to work and not that we've broken up. I suppose if I returned one of her million text messages, I would know this. We could at least be on the same page, but no, I'm left hanging on a lie, and I'm to blame.

Quinn sets this fork down and sighs. "Wanna tell me what's going on?"

I shake my head and move the food on my plate around to make it look like I'm eating. Looking over at Quinn is a mistake. His gaze bores a hole into my façade.

"My sister is acting weird and so are you. Spill and eat. You look like you've lost a ton of weight."

"There's nothing to say," I mumble.

"Clearly, there is." He stands and takes his plate into the kitchen. The silence is nice, but I know it's temporary. Quinn returns with another full plate and two bottles of beer. He sticks one in my face, and I reluctantly take it.

"Drink up."

"Getting me drunk isn't going to make me open up."

He chuckles and takes a sip of his. "Look Ben, you missed Christmas and that was a huge red flag, worse than missing the Super Bowl. Elle hasn't said boo. She has the same excuse, 'you're working' which is clearly a lie, so you can either get drunk and tell me everything or you can do it sober. In my experience, liquid courage is nice. It softens the emotions."

He's probably right. I lift the bottle and take a sip, and then another until half of it is gone.

"So, what did my sister do this time? I know she can be bratty and headstrong, especially when it comes to work. I also know she hides her emotions, but when it comes to you, she's genuine."

I hang my head, mostly in shame. She didn't really do anything, other than want to spend Christmas with her family, and was not willing to set a date to get married when I demanded she do so.

"It's not really something she did," I tell him. "I don't even remember how it all started, except I asked that we set a wedding date and she said we would, but not until after she got these new bands off the ground and your tour started." I shrug and take another drink. "I pushed the issue. I told her I didn't want to be like your parents. She took offense, which she had every right to do because Harrison and Katelyn have made it work for a long time. Anyone would be lucky to have a relationship like theirs. Except, I want more, and I told her so. I pushed and pushed until I said some things I can't take back."

Quinn is quiet and when I look over at him, he's staring at the ground. He finally inhales and reaches over to pat me on the back. "Elle loves you, Ben. I'm sure you can work this out."

I shake my head. "I don't want to work things out, Quinn. I want our relationship to be a priority and it never will be, not with her career. And the things I said needed to be said, and part of me isn't sorry I finally said them." I relax against the couch, fully expecting Quinn to get up and leave. He'd never turn against his sister, and I can't ask him to take sides.

"I told her I was done, and I meant it," I say without him asking. "It was the hardest and yet, easiest thing I've ever said to her. My heart is broken, but I know I'm better off."

Quinn sighs. "What are you going to do?"

"I don't know. Right now, I'm mooching off Elle and I

need to stop. I can't expect her to continue to support me. I don't deserve her kindness. I need to find a place to live, and it's probably not going to be in California. This place is too expensive."

"You can come stay with Nola and me. We have the space, and you can keep Nola company while I'm on tour."

"She's not going with you?"

"She's going to come to a few of the shows, but she's going to start working on her master's degree."

"Does it bother you that she won't go on tour with you?"

Quinn laughs. "No. No one wants to spend hours upon hours traveling by bus or living with other people. The rooms are small, the bus smells after the third day, and we spend more time sleeping than anything. I don't blame her one bit. I'll miss her but seeing her when she is there will be worth it. Besides, she's her own person and doesn't need to be at my side all the time."

"Maybe that's why Elle never asked me to come along."

"Maybe," he says. "But you've been on tour before, you know what it's like. I hate it after a few days."

"Tell me about the Super Bowl."

Quinn goes into everything I missed, and how people asked about me. He tells me about Oliver and how cute he is, and how Katelyn and Harrison are hoping to adopt him. Quinn hands me his phone and tells me to scroll through the photos. I do, pausing when I get to a picture of Oliver and Elle. Elle beams in each photo and it makes me wonder if she misses me at all. Are the text messages she's sending business related or is she telling me to get the hell out of her house? This entire time I thought the messages were her telling me she missed me. By the looks of these photos, she's not missing me at all.

Quinn stays for a couple of hours and when he leaves,

he tells me he'll be over this weekend to watch the basketball game, something we've done for years. I want to think he's not going anywhere, but the truth is, I've closed the door on this part of my life and he's going to eventually side with his sister. Eventually, Elle will move on and being friends with the ex will be frowned upon.

It's been days since I've showered and know if I'm going to start healing, I need to take care of myself. I finally drag my ass into the guest bathroom and turn the water on. I hate this bathroom, but it has zero memories of Elle, of us together. It doesn't smell like her shampoo or show me the things she's left behind. It's easier to be in here.

The hot water rushes over my skin, burning my flesh. I welcome the pain. It's easier to let this type of hurt wash over me versus the heartache I feel constantly. When the water temperature starts to change, I wash my hair and lather my hands with soap. Every inch of my body hurts from the water burn, but suddenly I don't care because there's something on my body that shouldn't be there.

It's a lump and it's hard.

# 5

# ELLE

*J*ustine paces in the hall and wrings her hands together. I've never seen her like this—on edge and agitated. Usually, she's the cool, calm, collected type, and has the biggest smile on her face. There's something definitely wrong, and with Plum about to go on stage, I need to figure out how to fix whatever the issue is.

I slip my hand over her arm and tug her lightly toward Plum's dressing room. Before I can close the door, a crew member from the show stops me. "They go on after the commercial break."

"I'm aware. We'll only be a moment." I shut the door and twist the lock to give us as much privacy as we need and turn toward Justine. Her chin-length hair sits high on top of her head in a ponytail and the blonde is now purple. Wynonna and Priscilla dyed theirs as well—something the three of them didn't tell me about until I saw them this morning. Of course, they hadn't needed to actually utter the words, "we dyed our hair" because the evidence was right in front of my face. I don't know how I feel about it and told them we can discuss it later. Their band's name is Plum, but that doesn't mean they have to embrace it.

"What's going on? Are you nervous?"

Justine shakes her head and then nods. "Yes, and no."

Yep, it's clear as mud now.

"You've performed before. Is it because we're on national TV?"

"Do you remember when I told you I had run away at fourteen?"

I nod and study her face for any sign she's about to throw a wrench into things.

"I'm scared my dad will see me on TV and try to come find me."

"Was he abusive?"

Justine looks into my eyes and then at the ground. She doesn't need to tell me anymore. I step closer and place my hands on her shoulders. "If we hear from him, we'll take action. For now, let's go out there and perform. Show the world who Plum is. Okay?"

She sniffs and mutters a very quiet thank you. I don't pretend to understand what her life was like when she lived on the streets. I can't imagine having a parent who mistreated me to the point where I felt my only option was to run away. For Justine to be in that situation, especially at fourteen, and persevere to where she is now—it's remarkable.

Justine and I head back to the hall, where Wynonna and Priscilla are waiting. A different crew member tells the girls to follow them. I trail behind, unwilling to let them navigate their appearance all on their own. Faintly, I can hear Helen of the *Helen Show*, talk to the audience about Plum, and how they were discovered at Trixie's (slight exaggeration)—one of the oldest bars in Hollywood—during an open mic night. I'm thankful Quinn and I were there that night because I have a feeling Plum is going to make it big. Their recently released single is already climbing the charts, and Dana Cantu from Sinful Distraction has approached me about writing songs for the girls. As a manager, when my bands come together to create music, it's magical.

The curtain lifts, and Priscilla is right on cue with the first note. I watch as her drumstick taps the snare, and then Wynonna comes in on bass. Justine steps up to the mic and, for one brief moment, I wonder if she's going to freeze. Her fingers strum the guitar strings, she opens her mouth, and the melody comes out.

Justine sings "Last Day"—Plum's hit song. It's the one Quinn and I heard her sing when we saw her at Trixie's. As soon as the girls signed their contract, I had Justine record an acoustic version as a bonus track on Plum's EP. It's a heartbreaking song about how you can lose everything but come out smiling at the end. The more I listen, the more I come to realize Justine is singing about her own experience, and while the song is sad, there isn't anything sad about her life now. Plum is going to go places.

Plum nailed the musical version of "Last Day" I put on all the streaming platforms. Within a day, they had over a million downloads and radio stations lit up my phone line for interviews. The media tour the girls are embarking on is very similar to the one Sinful Distraction did when they first started. Only, I have a bit more experience this time, and I'm not afraid to ask for more when it comes to my bands.

Justine ends the song. Everyone in the audience is on their feet, clapping. Helen walks over to Justine, places her arm around her shoulders and tells the cameras the name of the song Plum played and where to find their music. As soon as they go to commercial break, Helen heads toward me.

"I know it's not planned, but I'd like to interview the girls. I have a pre-recorded segment we can cut after the commercial break if they're willing."

"Of course." I lean slightly and glance at the girls, who seem extremely giddy with excitement. "They'll love it." Helen thanks me and as soon as she's gone, the three girls squeal and come to me.

"Oh. My. God!" Priscilla says as her hands go to her head. "We're going to be on TV."

"You already were," I point out, even though I know what she means. "Helen is going to ask you some questions. Some may get personal. You've seen her interviews before, so you know what to expect."

"She's going to ask if we have boyfriends," Wynonna says.

"Do you?" I question.

Wynonna gives me a one shoulder shrug to match the smirk on her face. I focus on Justine, leaning in and asking, "Are you okay with the interview?"

"You'll protect me, right?"

"Always," I tell her. "We won't let anything happen to you." As soon as she turns toward the others, I pull my phone out to leave myself a note: *Security for Justine.* Thankfully, she's of age, as are the sisters, but that doesn't mean Justine's father won't come looking for his piece of the pie. I've heard stories, and most rarely turn out well.

A crew member helps the girls put their mics on and then shows them where to sit. I stay backstage where I watch the show. After the commercial break ends, the camera pans over the girls, and Justine looks nervous.

"Wow," Helen says to her audience and the cameras. "Wow!"

The girl's giggle, and it's heartwarming to see their innocence.

"I'm sitting here with the gals from Plum: Justine, Wynonna, and Priscilla. First, I want to start with Wynonna and Priscilla. I read your parents named you after two iconic women. Is this true?"

"Yes," Wynonna says. "Our dad is named after Johnny Cash, and our mom is Patsy. I guess it was only fitting they'd name us something musical as well."

The audience laughs.

"Now, your single "Last Day" went live over a week ago and went right to number one on all streaming platforms. How have things changed for you since?"

"Other than performing for you and doing interviews, our teachers are still giving us homework," Priscilla says. "Maybe you can write a note for us?"

Everyone laughs this time. "I'll see what I can do," Helen says.

"What's it like writing your own music?"

"Cathartic," Justine says. "To transform your thoughts into a song and add a melody to them—it's the best feeling in the world."

"Well, your fans definitely agree." Helen has a screen behind her that shows Plum's cover. The three girls stand on the street, with a car behind them. The photographer laid down on the ground to capture the image. It gives the sweetest girls I know, edge.

Helen sends her show to commercial break and the girls exit the stage. I wait for them in the hall, and we all go to the green room. It's a quick decompress session, and then we're heading out the door and into the stretch Escalade.

"Did we do okay?" Justine asks.

"You girls were amazing." My phone beeps and I look at the screen. The Instacart order I placed for Ben has been delivered. I do not know if he's eating the food or not, but I know he won't go out and shop for himself. He hates the grocery store, and even shopping on the apps. Ben always deferred that task to me.

As soon as we get back to the studio, the girls grab their things and meet Johnny and Patsy in the waiting room. As much as they wanted to come with us, there aren't a lot of plus ones added to a nationally televised performance.

When I get to my office, I find Quinn sitting at my desk. "Don't even think about it," I tell him as I hang my coat up.

"You have no idea what I'm thinking."

Pfft. "I can only imagine. Scoot."

He reluctantly gets out of my chair and sits in the one across from me. I start up my computer and wait for my emails to load. Plum has more media requests, and a new email says URGENT—TOUR.

"Fuck," I mutter.

"What's wrong?"

I shake my head and open the email. After scanning quickly, I tell Quinn, "Loving Light wants Plum to tour with them."

"That's good, right?"

"It's amazing. It means we need to hurry and finish their album, but yeah. This is going to be huge for them."

"Let me know if I can help."

"I'm definitely taking you up on that. We have a few songs that need some background vocals, and they could use another guitar. Dad is coming in to work with Priscilla on her technique, and Dana wants to write a song with Justine.

Plus, I have Talking Til Dawn coming in to start their record. Grandpa is right. I need help."

Quinn chuckles. "As if you'd let anyone take over. You're a control freak."

"Liking things done a certain way doesn't make me a freak." I throw a wadded piece of paper at him. "Anyway, what are you really doing here?"

"Nothing," he says with a small shrug. "Just thought I'd stop in and see how you're doing."

"No complaints," I tell him. "Have you seen Oliver lately?"

"No, you? I feel like Mom is hiding him from us."

I can't help but laugh. Our mother isn't hiding the baby. She's probably plotting on how to use Ollie to convince us all to have our own babies. "Did you get him a surfboard yet?"

Quinn beams and sits up. "It's so freaking cute. I had to special order his wet suit and because he's growing, I ordered one in each size. I'm heading out there this weekend to take him out. You and Ben should come."

The mention of Ben's name gives me pause, but I hope I'm able to keep my emotions hidden. Quinn doesn't know about Ben and me, and I don't plan on telling him or anyone in my family for the time being. Ben and I need to sit down and talk. "Yeah, we'll be there. Ben started a new job, but he should be able to break away for a bit."

"Yeah, what's up with the new job?"

"Better benefits," I say. "The freelance work is good because he can set his own rate of pay and hours, but no benefits. Everyone needs health insurance."

"Ain't that the truth?" Quinn stands and makes his way to the door. "When do you need me in the studio for Plum?"

"Tomorrow. Is that okay?"

He nods. "When is Sinful Distraction recording?"

I flip through the calendar on my desk and rattle off the dates to him. "Will you be ready?"

"Yeah. Ajay is bringing Jamie and the kids out to mom and dad's this weekend. Evelyn wants to play with Ollie."

"Are Peyton and Noah coming over as well?"

"Dunno, I suppose. See ya."

"Bye." As soon as the door latches, the tears fall. I cry hard, holding my head in my hands. I don't have much time to cry out my emotion as there are voices outside my door, causing me to stop. I'm at work and need to be as professional as possible. After a couple of deep, calming breaths, I wipe my tears with my fingers and get back to work. As much as I'd love for Ben to join us this weekend, I know he won't. This just means I'll have to come up with another excuse. I don't know how much longer I can keep the secret from my family. My parents are already suspicious. It's only a matter of time until someone shows up at our house— *Ben's* house—and notices I'm not there.

# 6

## BEN

*H*ealthcare is a joke. I completely understand that everyone thinks their issues are the most critical ones because let's be honest, they are. However, when someone calls their primary care doctor and says, "hey, I think I found a lump on my testicle," you'd think the office would squeeze you in for an appointment.

Nope.

It's been two weeks since I found the lump, or what I think is a lump. Fourteen agonizing days of what amounts to me playing with myself, checking to see if it's still there and trying to mentally measure the damn thing. Apparently, if it's under pea size, I don't need to worry . . . as much.

The waiting room chairs are uncomfortable. I sit. I stand. I pace. I read every display case, pick up every magazine, and read the jokes in Reader's Digest. Every time I sigh heavily, the receptionist gives me a warning. I'm probably on her last nerve being as I'm on my own, but I'm too young for this shit. To me, this is an emergency, and could affect my entire life in ways I don't even want to imagine.

Finally, after a couple more dramatic sighs and some severe eye twitching from the receptionist, the nurse calls my name. She makes idle chit chat until we get to the scale. I stand on it and watch her fumble with the weighted dials. The nurse looks at my chart and then makes another adjustment.

"It looks like you've lost some weight."

"Isn't that a good thing?"

Without making eye contact, she says, "Not in your case."

And what case is that, exactly?

I'm sick?

Depressed?

Should I tell her I'm not eating because I've broken up with the love of my life, and while I'm the one who said things are over, I've been miserable since Elle left? Or should I say that since finding the lump, all I've done is drink beer to numb the thoughts running through my head?

I choose to nod, step off the scale, and follow the nurse to the examination room. She tells me to sit in the chair while she adds the blood pressure cuff to my upper arm. Every so often she glances over and smiles.

She's noted my blood pressure, which I guess is normal, since she had nothing to add. "Any recent life changes?"

Does the copious amount of alcohol I consume count as a life change?

"I guess. I'm not sure what constitutes a life change."

"Lost job? Relationship status?"

Wow, going for the juggernaut.

I rub my hands over my legs and think about how much I should tell this woman. I should keep some part of my life private, even though I know once Elle is photographed without her ring on, everything about me will be front and center on Page Six. The break-up will be my fault, of course, and the headlines will be something along the lines of how I couldn't hack it in her world. The editors won't be wrong, but they're not necessarily right either.

"My fiancée and I recently split. Things have been a bit rough, which likely equates to my weight loss, and then I found the lump." I can't look at the nurse when I say this and can only hear her typing away. "Oh, and I quit all my freelance jobs and took a corporate one for health insurance, which I guess is a good thing."

The nurse and I look at each other at the same time. The discernable frown on her face gives me pause. Something I've said isn't sitting right with her. I'm afraid to ask what's wrong because I'm not sure I want to know.

"The doctor will be in shortly. Undress and put the gown on, open in the front. You can leave your socks on." She gets up and leaves.

"Just my socks. Got it," I say to the empty room. Before I change, I glance around the room, missing the days when my pediatrician had dinosaurs and the ABCs for the border wallpaper. Now, it's dated flower wallpaper which has muted in color over the years. Same with the wall paint. It was probably stark white, but now it's dingy and yellowing. No amount of bleach is going to save it.

I undress, put the gown on like a bathrobe, and sit on the crinkly paper. This stuff is supposed to protect people from germs, but I don't see how a roll of very thin paper can do that. While I sit there and wait, I count the flowers. I get to forty when the door opens and my doctor walks in.

"Hi, Benjamin."

*Benjamin.* My name, and yet no one ever really uses it. "Hi, Dr. McNally."

McNally is probably Harrison's age, with a full head of

gray hair. We're about the same height and he's been my doctor since I moved to California for college. Other than that, I know little about the man, except I think he's good at his job. He holds my chart in his hand, reads today's notes, and then flips through to my other appointments and then back to the first. He frowns. This isn't a good sign. He sets it down on the counter and takes a seat on the stool.

McNally clears his throat. "You found the lump two weeks ago?"

"Yeah, and I called the next morning. Today was your first available appointment." It's a little jab, but he should know how anxious I've been and didn't want to wait—not for something this important.

He nods, stands, and tells me to lie back. This is the uncomfortable part: the examination. He pushes and asks the same question repeatedly. "Does this hurt?"

"Nothing hurts," I tell him. "I found the lump while showering. I feel fine, mostly."

"What doesn't feel fine?" he asks as he continues his assessment of my body.

I shrug, not that he's looking at my shoulders or my face. "Just not dealing with a break-up very well, and now this."

"Have you been eating?" he asks. "I noticed a considerable decline in your weight."

"Not really."

McNally pulls his hands away, takes his gloves off and tells me I can sit up and close my robe. I do as instructed and wait while he writes something down and types on the computer in the room. "I'm ordering some tests. They need to be done today. If you have plans, please cancel them. You're going to be here for a while. As far as your weight loss is concerned,"—he turns and looks at me—"the questionnaire you filled out when you arrived shows you're dealing with some depression, which makes sense if you're going through a break-up. I'm going to prescribe you an antidepressant, and I want you eating. If I don't see weight gain by our next appointment, I'm going to put you on some supplements."

"Okay." What else am I supposed to say?

"Is there someone you can call to accompany you today?"

I shake my head slowly. "Not really." The only people would be Elle and Quinn, and neither of them need to know about this. Just another stab in the gut when it comes to my life—they're all I have.

*Had.*

"I'll be fine," I tell my doctor. "I can go down to the cafeteria and get something to eat."

He eyes me suspiciously and for good reason. "It's important, Ben." I nod and fight back tears when he stops and places his hand on my shoulder. "Get dressed. I'm going to send someone in. They'll stay with you during your testing. You don't want to do this alone today."

I say nothing out of fear. I'll choke on my words. As soon as the door closes, tears fall from my eyes. I don't wipe them away, there's no point. More follow. By the time the knock sounds on the door, I realize I've sat there and bawled my eyes out. I clear my throat and ask for a minute, and then dress hastily.

On the other side of the door is an older man in a UCLA ball cap. He smiles, extends his hand, and tells his name is John. "I'm a retired firefighter and volunteer at the hospital. Doc says you would like someone to keep you company today."

I didn't say that, but I can't stomach the thought of

turning this guy away. "I'm Ben. Dr. McNally is ordering me some tests for today and I can't leave."

"Yep, I gotchu. We're going to take the skywalk over to the hospital. I'll give you a tour of all the secret passageways, as long as you don't tell anyone, and then we'll hit the cafeteria for lunch. My favorite chef, Beulah, is working today, and she will make us whatever we want, whether it's on the menu or not."

"Nice perk."

"It's all about the charm," he says. "Are you ready?"

*Nope.* "Yeah."

John talks the entire walk to the hospital. He's popular and we stop often to chat with the people we run into. He introduces me each time, as his friend, and for some odd reason, this makes me feel like I matter. I like him instantly.

We start the tour in the basement. Not ideal, since this is where the morgue is. Thankfully, John only shows me the door and we don't actually go in there, even though he says he's friends with the staff. Not surprising.

He weaves us through a series of tunnels, which were used mostly back in the heyday of Hollywood to hide celebrities who came for medical care. This was long before tinted windows were a thing. John says even now, some celebrities use the tunnels to hide from the paparazzi, even though they're not allowed on the premises. They'll sneak in and use their phones or some other Inspector Gadget type device to capture the elusive proof.

Before we even make it to the cafeteria, my phone rings and I'm summoned to report to the lab to have my blood drawn, and then I'm to go right to ultrasound. Everything seems easy, yet my heart races with fear. John holds true to his word and stays with me through both my appointments, except he stands outside the ultrasound room during the procedure.

We finally make it to the cafeteria, where I meet Beulah, who makes me spaghetti and meatballs with garlic bread. John orders the same, and when our meal is ready, Beulah brings it out to us.

"I've never been served in a hospital cafeteria before."

"Oh, believe me, she doesn't do this for everyone. If she doesn't like you, she'll tell you she's busy and to scram. She's a feisty one, but I bring her flowers every week to make her smile, and those seem to do the trick."

"I'll remember that for next time."

John's fork stills. "Next time, huh? Are we going to make this a weekly thing?"

I shrug. "I'm not very optimistic."

"That's a shame. My daughter says you have to manifest the outcome you want. I want to grow a full head of hair, but that never seems to happen. She manifested her raise, though, so it does work."

I chuckle. "That's awesome."

"What do you do for work?"

"I'm in advertising. I focus mostly on brand management, graphics, and work directly with marketing on products."

"Fun job?"

"Meh." I shrug. "I love it, but it's not overly challenging until a diva client comes in and then it's like playing a game of hide and seek. How long were you a firefighter?"

"Thirty years. Best job of my life besides being a dad, of course."

"Of course," I say. "How's retirement?"

John sighs, but it sounds more like a groan. "Boring, which is why I volunteer here. At first, it felt like I was on vacation, but after a few weeks, I became stir crazy. I started working at an animal shelter, but after bringing home my third dog in as many weeks, I thought I needed to find something else. I knew a lot of the emergency room staff and one of them suggested I work here."

"Is this all you do? Show people around?"

"Nah," he says, shaking his head. "I'll pick up lunch for staff or deliver flowers to rooms. Sometimes I'm the greeter at the front desk or playing in the kids' room. Wherever I'm needed."

My phone rings and my heart sinks. I answer and tell the nurse I'll be right there. John and I clean up and make our way across the skywalk and into the building where most of the offices are.

"Want me to come in with you?"

His question gives me pause. I barely know this man, but in the short time we've spent together today, I like him. "I'd like that," I say.

The nurse takes us to Dr. McNally's office, and I brace myself for the news. If it was nothing, I wouldn't be here. I grip the arms of the chair . . . and wait.

By the time I get home, I'm numb. Nothing makes sense anymore. A knock on the car window startles me. Quinn stands there and motions for me to get out of the car. I do, but it takes a massive effort on my part.

"Hey." I'm nonchalant in my greeting, hoping Quinn thinks he didn't just walk up on me sitting in my car.

"What are you doing?"

"Just thinking."

"I was standing here for ten minutes, dude. What's going on?"

I shake my head and tell him to come inside. Every house on this road has cameras and listening devices. The last thing I want is for my neighbors to hear my business. Inside, I ask Quinn if he'd like something to drink. He asks for a water, and the bottles of beer mock me as I stare in the refrigerator. I'm not supposed to drink, but with what I'm going through, should I really care? I'm not sure I should.

I bring Quinn his water, and sit down. He twists the top, takes a drink, and then asks me again what's happening.

"I have cancer." Saying it aloud sucks just as bad as hearing it from my doctor. "Fucking cancer."

"What?" Quinn's mouth drops open and his eyes widen.

I stare down at my legs, unwilling to look at Quinn. "I found a lump a couple of weeks ago. The doctor ran some tests and it's cancer. Doc thinks it's at least stage two, whatever the hell that means. I have to go to an oncologist at the end of the week, and I'll have surgery. I don't have much more than that."

"Did you call Elle?"

Now, I look at Quinn. "Why would I? I don't want her pity, and I definitely don't want yours. I have enough to deal with. Elle left. We're done. This is my issue. It's not news you can share with others. That's the last thing I want. Hell, I don't even know why I told you, except I have a feeling you wouldn't leave me alone until you prodded the shit out of why I'm so fucking depressed."

Quinn stares, his expression unreadable.

"Fuck," I say. "I'm sorry. I didn't mean to unload on you. I'm just frustrated—"

"And scared?"

"So, fucking scared. I'm too young for this shit, man. They're going to take my testicle, limiting my chances of being a dad. Of feeling like a man. Like why? What did I do to deserve this?"

"That's not how cancer works," Quinn states the obvious. "If it was, the world would be rid of all evil."

"I know," I mumble.

"Do you have someone to go with you to your appointment?"

I shrug. "Maybe. I hung out with a volunteer today. He's pretty cool. Stayed by my side when I got the news and made sure I made it back to my car. He gave me his number and I'm supposed to call him when I know my appointment times, and he'll be there."

"What about your mom or brother?"

"I don't plan to tell them. Anytime I talk to her, she wants money. The last thing I want is for them to come here and live off me while I'm going through treatment."

"Makes sense. What about my parents? You can trust them to not tell Elle if that's what you're worried about."

I shrug. "That would feel odd. They're her parents, not mine."

"My mom doesn't think that way about you, Ben. You know this."

I nod, but I won't call them. I can do this alone.

"Nola and I will be there whenever you say the word. We'll take you to all your appointments, sit with you during chemo or whatever, just say the word. I have nothing going on."

"You have a career."

"Eh," he says with a shrug. "I have a best friend who needs my help. He's far more important than a couple of song lyrics on a piece of paper. There isn't a tour on the horizon, and aside from a few days in the studio to record, I'm free."

"Okay." I finally relent. "Thank you."

When Quinn gets up to leave, I walk him to the door. What I don't expect is the bear hug he gives me before he leaves. "You're like a brother to me, Ben. You're not doing this alone."

# 7

# ELLE

*E*very time I listen to the tracks recorded at Plum's session, I start to think I'm sitting on a gold mine. And then doubt creeps in. What if I'm not good enough for them or not doing right by them? They're going to be huge. They're going to be the girl group version of Taylor Swift, and I'm just starting out. I wonder if Ryan Stone felt like this when he became the youngest general manager of the Boston Renegades? Whether he felt he wasn't good enough? What if their stardom far surpasses what I'm capable of?

If my dad were here, he'd kick my ass for thinking so negatively. I'm supposed to manifest greatness. I'm supposed to only see the good in what's to come, but there's a nagging voice in the back of my head telling me I'm going to launch Plum's career and they're going to take off, leaving me in the wind.

I search for Plum's folder and once I find it, I open it and peruse the notes I've taken since meeting Justine. Plum had been playing at Trixie's for a few months, and no one talked to them at all. Quinn and I were the first—this bodes well for me—as long as I continue to do right by them. But what if the deal I get them isn't enough?

Sighing heavily, I close the folder and open my email. Each message I write is tailored to the right manager at the record label. Luckily, with 4225 West owning the studio where my office is, I have the luxury of using their producers. Not to mention, Quinn, who seems to be the jack of all trades when it comes to music. He can sing, play, and produce music. I swear he lucked out in the genes category. So did Peyton. Her skills and knowledge of football when it comes to dissecting the game are exceptionally good. My talent is finding musical artists. Where I struggle is making sure they're a top ten artist, nominated for Grammys, and getting soundtrack opportunities. I'm not there . . . yet. Uncle Liam says I'm on the cusp of breaking into the big leagues. Thing is, I don't want to be on the cusp. I want to be over the edge. I want my bands to have long and successful careers. Not only in their industry, but also with me. It would break my heart if one of my bands left me and found success elsewhere because that would mean I failed them, and that's the last thing I want to do.

After writing the first email, I copy the pertinent information, attach Plum's demo, and send it off. I try not to let the anxiety build more than it already has, but I can't help it. I believe in these girls, their sound, and the vibe they carry. Especially when it comes to Justine. There's just something about her . . . I can't quite put my finger on. Maybe it's the haunting way she sings a ballad, the way she closes her eyes and transports herself into the heart of a song. It's even the way light twinkles in her eyes when she's about to sing the middle 8, whether it leads to a key change or the crescendo that all the fans will want to sing along to. She has superstar written all over her.

Once I have sent emails to the labels, I reach out to the security firm 4225 West uses when on tour. I explain the situation with Justine and ask to set up a meeting so we can discuss what measures should be taken.

Next, I do an internet search on Justine. This isn't something I've had to do in the past, but I have this nagging suspicion something isn't right. She tells me she's eighteen, and if that's the case she shouldn't worry about her dad tracking her down. If she's a minor, I'm in trouble. She can't sign any legal documents without her parents, unless of course she's emancipated.

"Ugh," I groan and push my fingers into my temples. I want everything with Justine to be on the up and up, but I saw the fear in her eyes before she took the stage at *The Helen Show*. She was afraid.

My email dings and my heart races even though I know full well no one from the music industry will get back to anyone within minutes. Although, with the girls appearing on *The Helen Show*, there might be a scramble to sign them to a label. My eyes scan the new messages, and my heart does a double tap. A Sony rep has responded to my email. Of course, it's the same one who signed 4225 West, but in this business, you use your contacts. The next email is from Universal. Both labels want to meet the girls, and I let out a thank you to whoever is watching over me right now.

"Holy crap," I mutter to my empty office. "Within freaking minutes."

"You know—"

My hand covers my heart as I startle. Slowly, I turn at the sound of my brother's voice and find him leaning against the doorjamb, hands in his pockets, ankles crossed, and wearing a beanie. He looks so much like our dad; Quinn could play him in a movie if anyone ever did a biopic about the band.

"What the hell, Quinn? Ever hear of knocking or, I don't know, checking in with Debra to make sure I'm not on some important call? I could've been negotiating your next record deal."

"But you're not doing either," he points out. I throw a wad of paper at him and glare.

"What do you want?"

"Well, that's rude." Quinn saunters in and sits down in the chair across from my desk. He's rigid, unlike his normal posture of extending his long legs and slouching.

"What's wrong?" I ask. "Are you not feeling the tracks you did with Plum? Because you sound amazing, and the mix is perfect."

"No, that's not it," he says, but offers me nothing more.

"Let me guess, you want to go on this mini tour with the girls?" I lean back in my chair and contemplate. "You know, that's not a bad idea. Of the six songs on their EP, you're on three of them. You'd be a huge draw for them. It's just a handful of stops," I tell him.

Quinn seems to digest what I'm saying but starts to shake his head slowly.

"All right, I give up." I throw my hands up in exasperation. I hate this . . . game or whatever he's playing. "What gives?"

Quinn clasps his hands together and studies me. I cock my eyebrow, hoping to convey I'm in no mood for this cat and mouse game he's playing. Another ding, and I turn my attention back to my computer. As soon as I see who it's from, I click to open it and pray it's the answer I want.

"Yes," I say loudly, and fist pump the air. "Yes! Yes! Yes!"

"What is it?" Quinn asks.

"The three majors want to meet with Plum. I think we might end up in a bidding war."

"You know that's not always good," he says. Unfortunately, he's right. Sometimes so much money is thrown at artists, they never make it back before their contract expires. Putting Plum in a situation where they're going to struggle is not how I want to do business.

"I know. I'll make sure the girls are protected and they have a nice deal." I close the email and turn back to Quinn. "Did you and Nola break up?"

His gaze turns sharp. "Why would you ask that?"

"You're being weird and it's the only thing I can think of. If something was wrong with mom or dad, or even Peyton, you'd just tell me. All this weirdness," I pause and make a bunch of circling motions in the air with my finger, "is—well for a lack of a better word—weird."

"I know what I'm getting you for Christmas."

"What's that?" I ask.

"A thesaurus."

"Hardy har har. Spill or leave. I have work to do, and you need to be in the studio. Dana booked you guys in there. She said you're working on something?"

Quinn nods, and then clears his throat. "How's Ben? I haven't seen him around the office much."

At the mention of Ben, my heart seizes. I pray my expression remains the same, hoping I'm not giving anything away. I look down at my blotter and act like what's there is super important. "Ben's good. He took a corporate job before Christmas, remember?"

"And that's why he didn't come to the lodge for Christmas?"

It takes me a moment to remember my lie. There have

been so many over the past few months. I honestly thought once the holidays were over, Ben and I would be back together and this thing going on between us would be water under the bridge. Clearly, I've thought wrong. I'm about to say yes when I remember I told my family Ben wanted to see his mom. One of the worst lies of my life.

"No, he went to see his mom."

"Oh, right," Quinn says. "Odd, though. Ben's always spent the holidays with us."

I shrug and hope Quinn takes my hint.

"It's too bad he wasn't at the Super Bowl."

"I know." I continue to keep my eyes on my blotter and write down things I need to do. This is the second time Quinn has asked about Ben and I'm starting to wonder why. Surely, Ben would've texted and let me know if Quinn had been over. "Are you here to talk about Ben or to work?" I ask, avoiding eye contact.

"Elle," Quinn says my name softly and in a brotherly tone. I can't help but let my building tears spill over. I cover my face and shake my head. "Why?"

"Why what?" I ask, my voice muffled.

"Why the lies?"

"Because I thought this was a hiccup and we'd be back to normal already."

"Have you tried?" His tone is accusatory, and I look at him instantly.

"Have I tried? I try all the time but Ben," I pause and shake my head, "I don't want to talk about this right now, Quinn." I spin away and stare out my window. I don't have a view of much, but at least I can see outside.

"You need to go see him, Elle."

I shake my head, even though I doubt Quin can see me doing so. "I've tried, Quinn. For a while I texted him every day, and nothing. No response. I went over there to get clothes, and we fought."

Quinn appears in front of me and kneels. "Can I help?"

"Not unless you can set a date for our wedding," I tell him. "Or what would've been our wedding. A date is what caused all this crap between us. Ben says things are over. He says he doesn't want to see me so I'm giving him the space he needs."

"You really need to go see him."

"Why? So, he can remind me that I broke his heart because I won't get married at the courthouse? No thanks. I want a wedding where Dad walks me down the aisle. I told Ben I'm sorry everyone's schedules don't match up, and eventually they will if we keep looking at dates, but that isn't good enough for him. And even if we got back together, I don't think we should rush into marriage. Look at us."

Quinn takes my hands in his and looks at me with the sincerest gaze I've ever seen from him. "You *need* to go see Ben."

"I don't think I can. I literally feel ill thinking about not seeing him and then the anxiety kicks in. He doesn't love me, Quinn."

"I think he does, but he's hurting, and he needs you, Elle." I spin back to my desk and grab my phone. After unlocking it and pulling up Ben's texts, I show the screen to my brother. "Does this look like a guy who needs me? Does this look like a guy who wants to talk to me?" Dragging my finger over my screen, I show Quinn numerous messages from me that Ben hasn't answered. "He made himself very clear, and honestly, I'm done talking about it. He broke up with me over a date," I point out. "Maybe it's for the best." I go back to my desk and toss my phone down. "Leave, please. I have work to do and the constant badgering about my ex is giving me a headache. I know he's your friend, and honestly, I hope you remain friends with him, but Ben and I . . . he doesn't want to be with me."

I open the first email regarding Plum and start to type my response. I can hear Quinn moving around behind me, and when he lets out a heavy sigh, it takes everything in me to ignore him.

"Elle, if you take anything away from what I'm saying, take this—Ben needs you. You need to go out to the house and see him before it's too late."

The "before it's too late" part catches my attention. By the time the words register in my mind, Quinn is gone. As tempted as I am to go find him, I don't. He could mean nothing by it, other than he wants Ben and I back together.

*Or he could mean everything.*

# 8

# BEN

*A*ll my life I have considered myself to be fearless. On the very first vacation I took with the Jameses, Quinn taught me how to surf. I was a mess. I could barely sit on the board, let alone stand without falling off. I kept trying, and everyone kept teaching. Liam, Harrison, Elle, and Eden. It was a humbling experience learning from someone who was a little girl at the time, but it was her lesson . . . well more her board that allowed me to stand and ride a wave. The trick was the smaller board. Something I could easily navigate. Sure, I continued to fall but I persevered and learned how to surf like everyone else in my family.

Who were my family.

I hate thinking about the Jameses, the Westburys, and the Davises in the past tense, but the truth of the matter is they're not going to go out of their way to invite me to family functions or outings. Especially once Elle moves on, which I know she'll do. I expect her to. Once she does, I'll be an afterthought, despite Quinn telling me otherwise.

The waves of the Pacific Ocean roll onto the shore. It's

early in the morning and surfers wait for the perfect wave to ride back onto shore. My surfboard is next to me, with my ankle strap secured tightly. I decided to forgo my wetsuit this morning because what do I need it for? I've convinced myself that I'm dying because I have cancer.

I have fucking cancer.

And in all places . . . my manhood.

I no longer feel fearless.

Someone yells my name. It's my neighbor. He's a young kid and he designed one of the most popular video games and made a boatload of money. I only see him in the mornings though, because he's always holed up in his house, working on the software. Quinn and I play his game every now and again, but it's not really our thing.

Gill sits down next to me. He's the silent type and has admitted to me on numerous occasions he doesn't have a lot of friends. I get it. It's hard to find trustworthy people to keep in your inner circle.

"How's the gaming world?" I finally ask to break the silence.

"Competitive. I think I have to sue someone for copying my idea."

"Dude, that sucks."

"Yeah," he sighs. "Wanna ride?" he motions toward the surf.

"Nah, I think I'm a looker today. Not feeling it."

"I hear ya."

We're silent again, just the two of us watching the others surf. Some of the people out there really make it look so easy. I'm a novice at best.

"Hey, whatever happened to that surfer chick you and Elle hang out with?"

"Eden?"

"Yeah, her. What's she up to these days?"

I shrug. "Honestly, I'm not sure. Elle and I broke up."

"No shit?"

I nod, unable to answer due to a knot forming in my throat.

"Wow, I thought you two were in it for the long haul."

Same, but I realize I knew better. Deep down, I think Elle needs someone on her level, in her circle, and not the high school crush she realized she couldn't live without after I left.

"Damn, man. I'm sorry."

"Thanks. Life is definitely an adjustment without her around." I don't know what else to say. Do I tell Gill I have cancer? That I might not be around for a bit or I might end up moving because there's no way I can afford this house by myself, and Elle isn't going to let me freeload off of her?

"If you need to talk, come on over."

"Thanks, Gill. I appreciate it."

"My sister is always telling her friends there are a lot of fish out there." He points to the ocean. "I don't get it because who wants a fish? I thought we were all supposed to be frogs or some shit. Anyway, I'm sorry about you and Elle." He stands and shakes my hand. "Let's hang this week."

"For sure. Be safe out there."

"You too, man." Gill is on his board in a matter of seconds and paddling out into the surf. I wish I could do it— be brave. Be the person Elle pictures me as, but I'm not.

I'm weak.

I'm sick.

I'm alone.

I know I'm at a crossroads. I can get up, wipe the sand off my ass, and go deal with what I can deal with, or I can wallow in self-pity. I broke up with Elle and I did so for a reason. I need to accept it. She's reached out and it's about time I return one of her many messages. Sighing heavily, I finally stand, grab my board and head back to the house. I'll text Elle today and ask for a meeting. The thought makes me chuckle and shake my head. I need to schedule a meeting with my ex because of how busy she is. So, probably sometime in a month or so, she'll squeeze me in, and we'll figure out what to do with the house.

After I clean off in the outside shower, I head into my bedroom, put on some clean clothes, and make my way into the kitchen. When I bypass the mirror in the hallway, I have to do a double take.

"Fuck," I mutter as I look at myself. The bags under my eyes are so dark, I look like I have two black eyes. Did Gill not notice, or did he just not care? Despite being out in the sun for over an hour, I'm as pale as a ghost. Nope, strike that. My eyes are bloodshot, so I'm definitely a vampire. It's not even Halloween and my costume is ready.

*Great.* There is no way I can meet with Elle looking like this. She'll know right away something's wrong, and I have no intentions of ever telling her what's going on. I don't want her pity and that's exactly what she'll give me.

I finally make my way into the kitchen and stare into the empty refrigerator. Elle stopped sending groceries about two weeks ago. Can't say I blame her. Why spend money on someone who doesn't want you? The thing is, I want her, but not in the way she can offer. I need more from her than she's capable of giving.

The doorbell sounds and I groan. I hope it's Instacart, but it's very unlikely, and unless I order my own food, I'm not eating any time soon. Being single is for the birds. I open the door and my jaw hits the floor.

"What's wrong?"

"Um . . . nothing. What are you doing here?"

"There's something wrong, I can see it in your face." My mother steps in and cups my cheek. "A mother knows things," she says. "I had a feeling something was wrong and knew I needed to come. Now, tell me."

I say nothing as she lets herself in. She tugs an extra-large suitcase behind her. Great, she's planning on staying. It's a good thing Elle isn't here because there's no way in hell, she'd let my mom stay here longer than a day or two. They get along, but my mom has a different view of the Jameses, and it's not favorable.

"Please, come in," I mutter as I close the door.

"Doesn't Elle ever clean?"

This is why I don't do much with my mother. She's snide and doesn't treat Elle with much respect.

"It's not Elle's job to clean the house."

"Well, doesn't she hire someone?"

My head goes back and forth slowly. Thankfully, she can't see me because she's facing the couch.

"Where do I put my stuff?"

"Um, third bedroom on the right."

"It's clean, right?"

Cleaner than anything you live in. "Sure."

My mom disappears down the hall. I can hear her grumbling about something, but I'm too tired to care. She can't stay here; even though Elle's not here, my mom can't be here. She's going to end up saying something to piss me off and I don't have the energy to deal with her right now.

"So, where is the princess?"

"Work, I guess."

"What do you mean, 'you guess?'" She's not looking at me but rummaging through the stack of mail on my coffee table. Damn, she's nosy. "What's this?" She holds up the appointment card for my oncologist appointment tomorrow.

"It's nothing." I try to take it away, but she moves it to her other hand and out of my reach.

"I'm not dumb, Benjamin. I know what oncology means. This has your name on it. Why?"

I shrug and look at her. "Because I have testicular cancer and have to meet with the oncologist tomorrow to find out what my options are."

❦

TELLING my mom is one of the biggest mistakes of my life. No, that's not entirely true. I've made a lot of stupid mistakes recently, and this one is definitely moving to the stop of the list. I suppose I should be happy I have some support, but she hovers. She's nitpicky and asking questions I don't have the answers to or care to know. The why, how, when, and anything else she can think of just keep coming and I need her to be quiet.

*Why this doctor and not this one?*

*Why this clinic?*

*How did you get cancer?*

*When will this go away?*

*Did I read the reviews on the clinic? On the doctor?*

People in the waiting room look annoyed and I don't blame them. "Mom, please stop."

"I have questions. I'm allowed to ask them."

"You are, but not here."

She huffs and flips through one of the twenty magazines she bought in the gift shop. Well, the ones she made me pay for. Nothing like piling a bunch of things on top of the counter and then looking at your son expectedly. What a great feeling.

John walks into the waiting room and my mood changes. I'm happy to see him. I know we've just met but I feel like he's my only advocate right now. I introduce him to my mom, and he sits down next to me.

"It's good that you told your mom."

"I didn't have a choice, she showed up at my place and rummaged through the stuff on my coffee table."

Realization crosses his face, and he nods. My mother was an okay mom. She worked hard to keep a roof over our heads, but she was never motherly. She didn't care what Brad and I did, just as long as we didn't get arrested. When I started hanging out with Elle, my mom expected to be brought into the family. She wanted all the perks of being friends with the Jameses and was rather put off when I never invited her to things. On the few occasions she's been around Harrison, she's made a complete fool of herself.

My name's called and the three of us stand. "Oh, we don't need you," my mother says to John.

I shake my head. "John's coming. He's a friend."

"But—"

*But nothing.* With John next to me, I head toward the nurse. She smiles at us, greets John, and asks how I'm feeling. It's a hard question to answer because technically, I feel fine, other than the symptoms my mind has conjured up because my brain keeps telling me I have cancer.

We sit in the oncologist's office, and I stare at all his diplomas on the wall. There are so many, and it makes me wonder how he decided this was going to his line of work. When he comes in, he greets us, and sits down with a file in front of him.

"Ben, I've spent some time looking through your bloodwork and scans, and after consulting with a couple of my colleagues, we're on the same page in saying surgery is absolutely necessary, followed by chemotherapy and possibly radiation. We're going to remove both testicles and lymph nodes, and then start you on an aggressive treatment plan. We'll monitor with scans regularly to make sure this plan is working, and if it isn't, we'll change it."

"You're going to remove both of my . . ." I can't even bring myself to say the word.

Doc nods. "It's the best option. With that said, I've made you an appointment with our fertility specialists."

"For what?" I ask.

"For when you're ready to be a father," he says. "This treatment will affect your ability to have children."

"Oh, Elle isn't going to like this one bit," my mom blurts out. "Why isn't she here, anyway? And why didn't she come home last night?"

I close my eyes and lean my head onto my hand, dragging it over my face in frustration. I should've told her to stay in the waiting room while I dealt with this, but I didn't want her to make a scene.

"How soon can we get Ben into the fertility clinic?" John asks.

"They're waiting for his call. It's not something we force, but highly recommend. Ben, you're young and while children might not be at the forefront of your mind right now, they might be later. Is Elle your partner?"

"His fiancée," my mother says. "But she's busy, ya know. Her dad is famous and all."

"Mom, please stop talking."

"Just stating some facts. She should be here. Elle will flip if you don't have any baby making stuff left."

"Brenda, why don't come with me," John says as he

69

stands. "My friend Beulah makes the best apple pie on the planet, and I hear she has some in the cafeteria. Let's go grab a slice."

As soon as the door closes, I feel relieved. I bend over and inhale deeply, only for tears to form. "I'm sorry," I tell the doctor. "My mother is . . . I don't have words. She just showed up yesterday, out of the blue."

"And your partner?"

"We broke up. She doesn't know I have cancer."

"Well, that's certainly none of our business. You're our concern, Ben. You can harvest your sperm or not. It's your choice. Like I said when John asked, the clinic is waiting for your call. We're going to schedule your surgery for next week, so this gives you some time to make a decision."

"Thank you." I stand, we shake hands, and he gives me a stack of information for me to read through.

After I catch up with John and my mother, she and I head back to the house. Once there, she rants and raves about Elle.

"Mom, I need you to stop."

"Why? Can't she be bothered to be here for you?"

"I broke up with her, Mother. She doesn't even know I have cancer. Stop putting this on her or blaming her or putting her down."

"Well, you should tell her."

"I don't want her pity."

"But you do want her money."

I shake my head and head into my room. I lock the door behind me, put on my headphones and turn the music up as high as it can go. But even this doesn't stop my mother's voice from replaying in my mind.

# 9

# ELLE

or the entire drive to the house, I give myself a pep talk. If Ben's home, I'll go in under the guise that I need clothes for the upcoming tour. It's a valid excuse as most of my stuff is still there, but one he'd easily see through. The last vacation we took, I forgot to pack a bunch of essentials and went shopping when we arrived at our destination. He knows I'll do it again if it means avoiding confrontation.

I hate confrontation. Mostly, I hate fighting with him about our breakup. But we need to talk. We need to discuss our future. If we're done, we need to make it official.

As soon as I pull up to the house, I notice a truck in the driveway. Ben has company. This shouldn't surprise me, and in any other circumstance, I'd use the fact he has company to avoid the conversation we need to have and drive away. But, according to Quinn, I need to see Ben. If I go inside and find another woman . . . no, I can't think like that. He wouldn't bring someone here. Would he?

My mind swirls with scenarios as I make my way to the front door. It could be the housekeeper, although I canceled the service weeks ago. Maybe it's a friend from work, although Ben's never brought any of his former colleagues to our place before. It could be his brother, but again, inviting Brad over isn't something Ben does. He's always kept our lives private from his family.

I open the door and see clutter in the entryway. Work boots, trash bags, and a couple pizza boxes. I shake my head, wondering what in the hell Ben's up to. Those boots are definitely not his and my early guess about Brad being here is right when I hear him yell at the television. If Brad's here, it means they've been drinking and probably on a weekend-long bender.

As I enter the living room, two sets of eyes meet mine. Not only is Brad sitting on my brand-new leather sofa, in his freaking underwear, but their mother is eating nachos and wiping her hands on the armrest. I bite the inside of my cheek to keep from saying something incredibly insulting and remind myself that Ben and I are not together, and while this is a fact, we haven't made any decisions on what we're going to do with the house. My hands clench into fists and my resolve is about to shatter with each step I take. The beautiful marble floor has a layer of dirty clothes on it, and when I look toward the kitchen, I can see dishes piled on top of the counters.

"Give me the strength," I mutter to myself.

"Say something, sweetie?"

I smile at Brenda and fight the urge to tell her she has queso in the corner of her mouth. "No, I'm just going to go find Ben." I hustle down the hall and into his office. By the time I reach him, I'm so angry that I want to scream. I slam the door, but he's wearing headphones and can't hear. Instead of calling his name, I pull them off his head to get his attention.

His expression morphs from anger, to recognition, and then finally emptiness. He has truly given up on us and that breaks my heart. I point toward the door and shake my head. There are so many words on the tip of my tongue, but nothing seems to want to come out.

"What in the actual fuck, Ben?" I say through clenched teeth. "Our fucking house is a pigsty."

"I know."

"Excuse me? You know? And you're not doing anything about it?"

Ben takes his headphones from my hand and sets them down onto his desk. "What are you doing here?"

"Excuse me?"

He frowns. "I don't need a reminder that you paid for this place. Believe me, I haven't forgotten."

"I'm not reminding you of anything, Ben. I came home . . ." Calling this place home doesn't feel right, not in the state our relationship is in right now. "What are Brenda and Brad doing here? And why in the hell is your mom eating on my couch? And why isn't your brother wearing pants?"

"What does it matter?" he asks, in a nonchalant tone making me wonder if he cares about anything anymore.

"Uh, it matters because this is still my house too. Because we need to decide what we're going to do with it and if your family is going to ruin the marble floors, someone is going to have to pay for it, and we both know they don't have the money."

"Stop yelling," he says, even though I don't believe I raised my voice at all.

"Stop yelling? Are you serious right now? You're letting them ruin our stuff! We worked hard for our things."

"No, your dad did."

"Screw you, Ben!" I walk out of the office and into our

bedroom. I almost don't get into the closet; afraid he might have done something with my clothes. Thankfully, my side is untouched, while his is all over the floor. I'm afraid to step anywhere because I have no idea what might be hiding under his crap.

I head into the bathroom and am surprised to find it fairly clean. I expected to find a ring of filth in the shower, hair everywhere, and who knows what floating in the toilet. Still, this isn't the Ben I grew up with, and I'm pissed Quinn told me to come over. I pull my phone out of my back pocket and send him a text telling him how he sucks and about Brad and Brenda.

After I pocket my phone, I notice pill bottles on the bathroom counter for Xanax and Valium. "What the . . ."

"What are you doing?" Ben asks, startling me. I hold the bottles in my hand.

"What's going on? Why are you taking these?"

"It's none of your business."

"That may be, but I'm making it my business. Quinn told me I need to talk to you and for the life of me I can't figure out why. But I'm willing to bet it has something to do with these. So, tell me what's going on."

"Like I said, it's none of your business."

"It *is* my damn business, Ben. You look like shit. You've lost weight, haven't shaved in over a month. You aren't cleaning. Your mother and Brad are here, and my brother won't stop pestering me about coming out here. So, here I am, Ben, crying in front of you, begging for you to let me in because I still fucking love you. Please, tell me what's going on." I don't bother to wipe away my fallen tears. He needs to see them. Ben needs to see his words and lack of effort are hurting me. I didn't want this break up, he did.

When he doesn't say anything, I throw the bottle at

him. "Whatever, Ben." I brush by him and head back to what was once our shared bedroom.

"Fine, you want to know going on?" he yells. "I have fucking cancer, Elle. I have fucking cancer in my nut sack. Are you happy now?"

His words stop me dead in my tracks. Surely, I've heard him wrong. I turn slowly and look at him. "What did you say?"

"I have cancer," he says quietly. He looks down at the ground when he speaks, but I still notice the lone tear making its way down his cheek before he quickly wipes it away. "The pills are to help me sleep, and for anxiety." I walk closer to him and stand where he has no choice but to look at me.

"Ben," I say his name and then cover my mouth. I rest my head on his chest and he finally wraps his arms around me. "Oh, Ben."

"Don't cry, Elle."

As much as I want to stop, I can't. He's been my best friend for most of my life and this patch we've hit, it's been rough, but I never thought it would last. When Ben's grip on me loosens, I step back.

"When did you find out?"

"Not that long ago."

"Are you doing chemo or something?"

"Surgery first, and then chemo and maybe radiation."

"When is your surgery?"

"Next week," he tells me.

"Is this why your mom and Brad are here?"

He shrugs. "She just showed up and then she called him."

"Why didn't you tell me?"

Ben steps back. "Because it's my problem not yours, and we're not together anymore. Besides, I'm sure you're busy."

"Together or not, I love you. You're my best friend and there isn't anything I wouldn't do for you."

"Except set a wedding date."

"That's not fair, Ben, and you know it."

He nods and moves toward the counter to put his pill bottles back. He stares at me through the mirror. "Did Quinn tell you? Is that why you're here?"

"Quinn knows?" Of course, he does. I don't wait for Ben to answer before continuing. "Quinn didn't tell me. He came to my office the other day and told me I needed to come out here and see you. When I first walked in, I thought it was because he wanted me to see what a trash hole the house is, but now I know. He wanted me to come out here because you swore him to secrecy, and he kept your secret."

"I don't know why I told him. He's the first one to know. He's come over a couple of times. I can't figure out if he's trying to play peacekeeper between us or what."

"He's not," I tell him. "Quinn's your friend. He will always be your friend regardless of us."

"You say that—"

"I mean it, Ben. Quinn would never stop hanging out with you because we broke up, unless you did something unforgivable. What happened with us, is because of us or me or whatever. It's not like you cheated or hit me."

Ben rests against the countertop. "I know I can't afford the house on my own, and I know I shouldn't ask, but can we wait before we divide things up? I'm not really in good enough shape to move right now." I don't remind him that the house is paid for. It's something he should know. I've never kept it a secret that I used my trust fund to buy this place. Ben pitched in, but a house payment is something we don't have.

"I'm not going to kick you out. Your mother and brother on the other hand . . ."

Ben chuckles. It's the first time I've seen him smile since Thanksgiving. He turns and looks at his face in the mirror and groans.

"You're right, I look like shit." He runs his hand over his beard. "I'm not even a fan of this beard but I'm too lazy to shave."

"Sit down, I'll do it for you." I pull out his shaving supplies and nudge him toward my vanity. He sits as still as he can and allows me to shave him. When the razor drags over his skin, he swallows hard. "I'm almost done," I tell him. I thank my dad for this, for teaching me how to shave a man's skin. I don't know why he taught Peyton and I, but we loved sitting on the counter with him while he shaved. And then one day, he handed us the razor and held his hand over ours, guiding us. Peyton and I took turns learning how to shave his face. He never once complained about the nicks we gave him. Now, I feel like I could open my own barber shop and offer a fresh shave to people.

"Do you want me to trim your hair?"

He shakes his head. "I'm going to lose it soon. I want to keep it until it starts to fall out, and then I'll shave it."

"Yeah." I run my fingers through it, and he closes his eyes. "I'm so sorry, Ben. This is wholly unfair."

Ben looks at me and tears fall from his eyes. "I'm scared, Elle."

## 10

### BEN

*E*lle pulls me into her arms. This is where I want to be, but also, nothing feels right. I don't want her pity, which is why I didn't tell her to begin with. She's going to try and fix everything, when in reality, she can't fix any of it. Elle can't make the cancer go away. She can't stop my hair falling out. She can't stop me from puking my guts out due to the chemo.

But she's going to try, especially if I don't stop her.

I start to stand, gently pushing her away from me. Deep down, I know she cares about me but right now, having her here is too much. Had I known she planned to come over, I could've prepared myself better. I could've been on my A-game and when she started asking questions, the wall would've been up.

One look at her though, despite how angry and hurt I am over our relationship, and any resolve I had built for the past month slipped away. I love her and I'll undoubtedly love her until the day I die—even if that's sooner than I think.

"Where are you going?" she asks.

78

"I need some space," I tell her and head back to my office. She follows me, clearly not understanding what space means. When she gets to my office, she closes the door and starts to say something but her phone rings.

"Hello. Yes, that's right. Yes, it's a mini tour, US only. Yes, I'll be with them. Okay, call my office and set it up." She hangs up and gives me a soft smile. "Sorry about that."

"No problem," I say, shrugging. "Work will always come first. I know that now."

"Ben—"

I hold my hand up. "I get it, Elle. It has taken me a long time to realize where I fit in your life. I'm second on most days, third on the rest."

"That's not true."

"Isn't it? You put your job way before us. If your sister calls and needs something, you'll drop whatever you're doing to be there for her. And then there's me."

Elle huffs and wipes away her tears. "Your assessment is off. My job seems as if it comes first because I'm trying to build a career. I don't want to be a joke in this industry, and I definitely don't want some unsuspecting teenagers to end up with someone shitty managing them like my uncle Liam did. You have a career, Ben. I've never complained when you've worked late or had to fly to San Francisco for meetings. I never complained when you were late for dinner or had to cancel because your boss needed something from you at the last minute. You could've quit and come to work for me full-time, but you insisted on being separate from me. You want to blame me for failing in our relationship, but there are two of us here. I'm not the only one who didn't give one hundred percent. I'm sorry, but you don't get to wake up one day and decide things need to work differently between us. Don't act like you're innocent in all of this. We agreed on a timeline for our wedding, and suddenly you want to rush it. As for my sister, you don't understand the connection and I can't explain it."

Elle paces the room, rubbing her arms. Every so often she looks at me, waiting for me to say something. I'd like to, but I have no idea where to even start. She's not wrong, but she's also not right, either.

"Did you know you had cancer back in December or sense something was wrong? Were you sick then?" she asks.

"What kind of question is that?"

"The kind that makes sense on why you suddenly wanted to set a date. Did you know?"

I shake my head slowly. "I didn't know until two weeks ago. I was in the shower and felt the lump. I called my doctor the next day and it took them two weeks to get me in. He suspected it was cancer and sent me for a bunch of tests."

Elle leans against the wall. There's a loud crash in the other room and she stands tall, pointing toward the door. "They have to go."

"You want me to kick my family out while I'm battling cancer?"

"No, but they can't stay here. They're trashing our house."

"They're my family," I point out.

"Since when? You've spent most of your life living as if my parents are your family."

"Things change."

Elle rubs her temples in frustration. "Look, Ben. I know you're going through the unthinkable, but since when do you depend on your mother for anything? Brad, I understand because he's your brother. But your mom? For as long as I've known you, you've kept her at arm's length."

"So, now when I need her, I should push her away?"

"That's not what I'm saying."

"Then what *are* you saying?"

"You didn't invite her. She didn't know prior to getting here about you having cancer. Her arrival is suspect."

"Well, she's here."

Elle sighs. She opens the door and heads down the hall. It takes me a moment to realize what she's doing, and I chase after her.

"Don't, Elle."

"Don't, what?" She spins so fast, her hair whips around.

I say nothing because I know she's going to speak to my mom whether I want her to or not. This is Elle's house, and she could kick us all out, although I suspect she wouldn't do that to me.

"Why are you here?" she asks my mom.

"My Benny needs me."

Elle scoffs. "Why. Are. You. Here?" Every word is enunciated.

My mother looks from me to Elle and to Brad, who focuses on the television. Oddly enough, he's still in his underwear, and as I look around, I can definitely understand why Elle is upset with them being here. They're acting like pigs because they expect Elle to pay for a housekeeper.

"Why, Brenda?" Elle asks again. "Of all the years we've lived in this house, you've never come to visit. So why now? Why did you randomly show up here?"

Mom looks sheepish and I know I should step in, but now I'm curious as well. I don't know why I didn't press her about her arrival earlier. I guess I was too concerned about what I'm going through to think anything of it.

"I lost the house," she mutters quietly.

"And you thought you'd show up and just—what—free-load?" Elle gives me a pointed look and then heads back down the hall.

"She needs to get off her high horse," Mom says. "This is your house too. Little Miss Money acting all high and mighty because her daddy is rich. She should be thanking me for being here since she can't be bothered."

"I broke up with her, Mom. Not the other way around."

"Shouldn't matter. She has the money to take care of you and what's she doing, running back to wherever she came from."

"She's not running. She has to work."

"Oh, please. She doesn't work. Her daddy does every-thing for her."

I look down the hall when I hear things slamming. Elle's pissed which doesn't bode well for anyone. I glance back at my brother, the living room, and the mess he and mom have created. "Clean this up," I tell them. "You may want to live like shit, but I don't. And put some fucking shorts on, Bradley. People sit on the couch, and they don't need to sit in filth."

Before I can make it down the hall to see what Elle's doing, she comes storming toward me with a suitcase drag-ging behind her. She doesn't say anything to me as she passes by. I follow her outside and take her suitcase before she drags it down the stairs.

"How much of that did you hear?"

"All of it," she says without making eye contact.

"I'm sorry."

"You're not, so don't even say you are. You didn't defend me, so clearly you think I just live off my dad's money. Which means you do too."

Once the liftgate on her SUV is open, I set her bag in there. "She's always been this way."

"Yep," Elle says. She presses the fob, and the back closes. "And yet, you've never put up with it until now. I get it. I'm the bad guy." She shakes her head and turns away from me so I can't see her tears. "Can you send me the date of your surgery so I can be there?"

"I'll be fine, Elle."

"Right." She gets into her car and starts it up. I wait for her to roll down the window, but she doesn't. She pulls away and I stand there, watching her drive down the road. I have a feeling this is the last time I'm ever going to see her.

# 11

## ELLE

*T*he drive to my parent's house takes longer than normal. I have to pull over a couple of times when my emotions get the better of me, and my eyes become too blurry to drive. I keep imagining Ben living a healthy life after this battle, but as soon as I see him happy and smiling, the vision changes and I see me standing next to his hospital bed, begging him to hold on. I can't lose him, and yet I already have, and I don't know what to do to get him back. He seems resigned on ending us, and it's not going to matter what I want or what I have to say.

I didn't call my parents to let them know I'm coming out, so I'm not shocked they're not home. I use my key and go into the condo, and head to what used to be mine and Peyton's room. It's now Oliver's room and smells like baby. I pick up his teddy bear and hold it to my nose, inhaling deeply. I let the tears flow as I hold the bear to me.

"Life isn't supposed to be this way." I sob. "Haven't I been through enough?"

I sit down in the rocker my parents have in Oliver's room and curl up. I don't remember my grandma, because she died of cancer when I was three or four. Then my father died, and I almost lost my soul when Peyton was in the car crash. Had I lost her, I don't know how I'd survive. She's part of me.

Ben, though.

I love him and can't imagine my world without him whether he wants to be my lover or my friend. I know that healing from a breakup takes time, but it doesn't seem like we have time to heal. Not with him being sick.

"Fucking cancer," I say to Oliver's wall decorations. "How can he have fucking cancer?"

God, I want to throw shit. I want to beat my hands against the wall, against the windows. I want to watch glass shatter and feel it rip my skin. I welcome the pain because then I'll know if I'm feeling or just being present. Ben thinks I'm emotionally stinted. He's probably right. I like to keep my feelings locked because feelings get exploited. People use your feelings against you in my industry. They call you weak if you show too much emotion. I need to be strong, resilient, and show every person who doubts me that I can make it on my own, without the help of my dad.

Ben doesn't need to see this side of me.

Another wave of fresh tears fall, and I do nothing to stop them. Eventually, I'll run out and there'll be nothing left. I want to be there for Ben, but he doesn't want me.

*He doesn't want me.*

He didn't ask me to stay. To help him. To be by his side. To hold his hand. To be there when he wakes up from surgery.

He says he'll be fine.

*Fine.*

He doesn't love me anymore.

The front door slams. I wipe the tears away and put

Oliver's teddy bear where I found it. My parents will know something's wrong as soon as they see me, and I'm not prepared to tell them.

I run into Quinn coming down the hall and all I see is red. I rush toward him, place both hands on his chest and push him backward.

"Whoa, what the hell?"

"Why didn't you tell me?" I hit him again, this time with my closed fist. "Why couldn't you just be my brother for once and tell me that Ben was sick.?"

He grabs my wrists and holds them away from his body. I squirm, trying to get out of his grip, but there's no use.

"Calm down, Elle."

"Screw you, Quinn."

He directs me toward the hall and pushes me away. "When you're an adult, we'll talk. Until then, go have your pity party in the guest bedroom."

"Oh, the high and mighty Quinn, bossing everyone around."

He stares at me for a moment and then shakes his head. "You're your own worst enemy, sometimes. I don't get it, Elle."

"Ben's sick and you kept it from me. If anything happens—"

"You'll what? Blame me? How in the hell is any of this my fault? Yes, Ben's sick. He chose not to tell you. That was his choice. Not mine, and certainly not yours."

"You don't get it." I walk toward him, leaving the confines of the hall.

"No, I do, Elle. You're used to everyone bowing down to you. You're the princess. You get what you want. Believe me, Elle. I know because I grew up with you." He stops and shakes his head. "When are you going to grow up and realize *this* isn't about you. It's about Ben. That's it. No one else. Not me. Not you. Not his brother. Ben needs to be the priority."

"Hey," our dad's voice booms from the doorway. "What in the hell is going on in here?" He comes into the living room with our mom behind him. She has the look of horror in her eyes as she holds Oliver on her hip. He smiles when he sees me and as much as I want to go to him, I can't right now.

"Elle, why are you crying?" Mom asks.

Neither Quinn nor I say anything.

"Someone better start talking right now."

"Ben's sick," I tell them. "He's got cancer."

"What?" Mom screeches.

"Tell them all of it, Elle. Stop lying to them," Quinn spits out.

"What's Quinn talking about, Elle?" Dad asks.

"Ben ended things the night before we met in Vermont for Christmas because I wouldn't set a wedding date."

"Wait, what? I think I need to sit down for this. I'm going to go put Oliver down for a nap." Mom passes by me, and I give Oliver a kiss on the cheek. I want to hold him, love on him, but right now he'd be an escape from my problems.

"Why were the two of you fighting?" Dad asks.

I eye Quinn, who stares back. "I pushed him and then hit him because of Ben."

"Explain," Dad demands.

"I knew about Ben, but he swore me to secrecy."

I look from my dad to Quinn and shake my head. Dad is going to agree with Quinn, and I don't want to hear it. I head toward the slider and don't stop when Dad asks me where I'm going. "I need to be alone."

I'm thankful my parents live on a private beach. It keeps people from loitering or using it as their own space. I get as close to the surf as I can and sit down. There are a group of surfers out there, waiting for the right wave to come in. I watch them for a minute or so, until my mind drifts off to memories Ben and I have shared over the years. From the time we first met, to becoming best friends, to prom, graduation, and moving to California. He's been my constant companion for as long as I can remember.

My parents sit down beside me, and more tears fall. They wrap me in their love and hold me while I cry. I tell them about the fight Ben and I had before Christmas and how I've lied about us being together because I didn't want to believe things were over between us. They let me tell my story, without interruption, and when I get to the part about Ben being sick, my mom cries.

"Oh, honey. I'm so sorry," Mom says as she comforts me.

"He's afraid I want to be like you guys and never get married." I look at my parents. "Like, what's wrong with the way our family works?"

"A lot of people don't understand why your mom and I haven't gotten married. This works for us. We're committed. We don't need a piece of paper to tell us what we already know. Besides, you don't see anyone hounding Goldie Hawn and Kurt Russell. They've been together for a millennium, and it works for them. However, it's not going to work for everyone. I can see why Ben wants to get married."

"You can?"

"Sure, honey. He didn't have a father growing up, and to him it shows stability within the family."

"That makes no sense, Dad. You didn't have a father growing up and you're not married. And Mom . . ." I glance at my mom, and she gives me a slight head shake. We don't talk about her family. They're different and chose not to be around when Peyton and I were growing up. Mostly, they didn't like my father, and when he died, my grandmother thought she could come around and be a part of our lives and my mom told her to take a hike. In the time Peyton and I grew up in Beaumont, the Cohens were rarely around. They showed up for a few birthdays or Christmases, but that's it. We have our grandpa and our grandma Bess. And sometimes, we have Bianca.

"I love Ben. I truly love him with my whole heart. I know that Peyton and Noah have something deeper, stronger, but that doesn't mean Ben and I aren't right for each other.

"You can't compare your relationship with Ben to Noah and Peyton's," Mom says. "They were destined to be with each other. I sensed it when I was pregnant with you both. She responded to his voice all the time."

"They're so perfect, it's hard not to compare."

"They're not as perfect as you think," Dad says. "They struggle, just like your mom and I do."

My eyes go wide at my dad's statement. "Bullshit!"

"Don't cuss, Elle," Mom chastises me. "And your dad is right. No one has a perfect marriage. Your dad and I don't always see eye-to-eye on things, and sure we argue, but at the end of the day, we love each other and find a way to compromise."

"I've tried with Ben, but he doesn't understand that I want you to walk me down the aisle," I say as I look at my dad. "That's important to me, and right now, our schedules don't match up. I told Ben we can pick a date, something attainable. He came back with "right away", back in December, and I told him no. And he wants kids. I do too, but . . ." I trail off. We want the same things; our timing is just off.

"Honey, Ben's feelings are valid," Mom says. "But so are yours. I know how important it is to have your dad walk you down the aisle."

"I just don't know what to do. I don't want to see him hurting like this, whether we're together or not."

"I know, sweetie." Mom rests her head on my shoulder. "We'll do everything we can to help him."

*Help him.*

I maneuver so I'm looking at my parents. "I can help him. I can make sure he has the best doctors in California. The best care available. I'll hire the best in home nurses, make sure he has whatever he needs. I'll do that for him." I start to get excited by my plan, but my parents don't react like I thought they would.

"What if Ben just needs you to be by his side? To be there when he wakes up from surgery?" Mom asks. "Sure, you can afford the best of everything, but sometimes what someone needs is the one they love the most."

"Mom's right, kiddo."

"Well, then . . ." I stare at the water, feeling helpless and frantically thinking of ways I can be there for Ben. A thought hits me and I throw my hands up in the air as a plan takes shape. "Dad, I need your help."

"With?"

"My new group, Plum. They're invited on a twenty-stop tour with Loving Light. US only. Would you be willing to go with them? I want to be there for Ben, and if I go on tour, I'm going to be a mess and won't be able to focus on the girls."

He looks at my mom and asks, "Are you okay with Oliver for a couple of weeks?"

Mom nods. "I have a feeling we'll be busy, making sure Ben is well taken care of."

"Does that mean you'll do it?"

Dad nods and I launch myself into his arms. "Thank you, Daddy."

"One condition," he says when I release him. He stands, helps my mom, and then me. We brush as much sand off us as we can.

"What's that?"

"Apologize to your brother. I've never seen you at odds like that with him. Ben is his friend too and Quinn kept his friend's confidence. You would've done the same thing."

"You're right. I'll talk to Quinn."

Dad puts his arm around me and the three of us walk back into the house. Quinn's on the couch, playing with Oliver.

"I thought I put him down for a nap?" Mom asks as she enters the room.

"Uh . . . he fussed," Quinn says sheepishly. I think everyone in the room knows this isn't true.

I sit down next to Quinn and rest my head just below his collarbone. When Peyton and I were younger, we'd each take a side, and the three of us would lie on the floor to watch movies. Quinn was, and will always be, our built-in pillow.

"I'm sorry for earlier," I say but realize I need to look at him. I sit up and meet my brother's gaze. "What I said and did, please know I didn't mean it. I'm frustrated and sad, and very, very scared."

"I meant what I said, Elle." His words shock me. "You need to grow up. If you're going to be there for Ben, be there fully. Don't half ass it and then get pissed when he tells you he doesn't want you around. If you love him, show him. Don't just throw money at someone because you think it's going to help. Be there for Ben."

"I'm going to," I tell my brother.

"How?"

"Well, regardless of what you think, I'm going to make sure his doctor is the best, because I love Ben and I don't want him to be in the hands of someone who doesn't know what the hell they're doing. I get that you may think I'm throwing money at the problem, but you'd do the same thing for Nola.

"Dad's going to go on tour with Plum so I can stay with Ben. I'm going to call Uncle Liam and ask him to help out in the office, and I'm hoping my brother can pick up some of my slack."

Quinn looks at Oliver and says, "I don't know, Ollie. Are you up for the job? Those musicians can be divas."

Oliver coos.

"Oliver thinks you should help out."

Quinn shrugs. "If Ollie says yes, then I'm in."

I hug Quinn and apologize again for what I did. After checking in with my parents, I tell my dad I'll send him all the info on Plum's tour and set up a time tomorrow for them to meet. Mom gives me a hug and tells me she'll be over to see Ben in the next day or two. I don't bother to tell her or my dad that Ben's mom and brother are at the house. I'm hoping to rectify that situation before Mom shows up.

## BEN

*I* don't know how long I stay outside, watching the taillights of Elle's car disappear down the road. It isn't until Brad comes outside and says we were out of beer, and he wants to order pizza that I realize I've been out here for maybe an hour or so. If Quinn had said this . . . well, he wouldn't have. He would've gotten in his car, gone to the store, stopped at the pizza parlor and returned with everything. Neither my brother nor even my mother can bring themselves to do such a simple task. Elle's right, they freeload. And they do so because of who her dad is, and that's not right. What makes this situation worse is I'm the sick one. I'm the one who is facing surgery—life altering surgery, plus the treatment that goes with killing the cancer cells—and my family can't even step up. They expect me to take care of them.

What a fucking joke.

When I get back inside, the mess I told them to clean up hasn't changed. Brad is rummaging through the refrigerator, mumbling something under his breath, and my mom is flipping through the channels on the television, while eating a bag of chips. I shake my head and wonder why.

Why do I put up with this?

Why do I need these people in my life?

Why are they like this?

Mom glances my way and smiles. Unfortunately, I can't return the gesture because I'm not happy. I'm not happy about my status with Elle, my life as it is now, my health, or my family. I hate to admit it, but Elle's right, my mother and brother shouldn't be here because they're not here to support me.

"Bradley, who's running your garage while you're here?"

He's moved from the refrigerator to the cupboards and slams the cabinet door. "When Mom called and told me you were sick, I closed up shop. I figured I needed to be here."

Is he really here for me though? He's not helping out around the house or making sure I'm okay.

"And you?" I ask as I look at my mom. "What about your job? I get that you lost the house and showed up here, aren't they expecting you at work?"

"Well, I lost that about three months ago," she says, as if it's no big deal.

"And you didn't find another one?"

"I applied around." She shrugs.

*Right, God forbid you get a job.*

"Well, I'm going to set some rules. If you don't like them, leave. I'm at the point in my life right now where I simply don't care."

Brad comes out of the kitchen and crosses his arms over his chest. "Don't be ungrateful, little brother."

I scoff and shake my head. "Here's the thing, if you're

going to stay here, you're going to pick up after yourself. Elle isn't responsible for cleaning or supplying you with food, and neither am I. This is our house, and we like it to be a certain way. Granted, when you arrived, it wasn't exactly clean, however that doesn't entitle you to be pigs."

"You listen to that girl way too much," Bradley says.

"It's because he's a whipped little boy," my mother cackles and Bradley follows suit.

"Laugh all you want, but this is her house as well. We haven't made any decisions on how to split it, and she has a right to be concerned. With that said, I have a feeling she's gone to her parents and told them about my diagnosis, which means Katelyn is sure to come over and Harrison will too, eventually. This place needs to be cleaned and done so now. Not to mention, the germ infestation isn't going to be good for my recuperation."

"I don't have germs," Brad says.

I roll my eyes. "Everyone has germs, you dumbass." I head toward my office knowing they're not going to clean. They may start, but something will come on the television and their attention will be elsewhere. Back at my computer, I pull up the website Elle and I have used for housekeeping and request some services. It's not something I plan for, but the house needs to be cleaned before I come back with a compromised immune system. After I complete the booking, I put my headphones on and return to work. I need every distraction possible and need to not think about what's going on in my body or my heart.

Truth be told, it was good to see Elle today and to hash out our issues. I'm not dumb in thinking things will change between us, because I know they won't. She is who she is, and I am who I am. We're like oil and water, we like each other but don't mix well. Which just really sucks because I love her. I've loved her from the moment I laid eyes on her, without knowing who she was.

The computer screen blurs, and I find myself crying once again. It happens every time I think of Elle and what could've been. Part of me thinks the smart thing to do would be to take her back but doing so doesn't solve the issues around us. And taking her back now makes me look like I need to depend on her and makes her look like she only came back because I was sick. Neither of us need that kind of pressure.

My phone rings and when I glance at the screen, I see my doctor's name and number. My heart drops to the floor and stays there. I swallow hard and my shaky finger presses answer and then hits the speaker button. "He . . ." I stop and clear my throat. "Hello?"

"Ben? This is Dr. Dowling. The surgeon had a cancelation and I'd like to move your surgery up to this Thursday."

Do I want to ask why someone would cancel surgery? Did his patient die? Miraculously recover?

"Um . . . okay?" Thursday is two days away. The day after tomorrow, I'm going to be cut open and have parts of me removed.

"Excellent. I'll have the nurse send over your pre-op instructions." He hangs up, but I have questions. Mostly, why?

Why me?

I head out to the living room to tell my mom the date of my surgery has been moved and find it somewhat clean. Thankfully, they're still working, and I decide against interrupting them. I guess my little tirade hit them where it counts. Before I can retreat to my office, Elle walks back in.

She stares at me, the cleaning supplies on the floor, and then makes eye contact with my mother. I expect a full-on fight, but Elle gives a small smile and then looks at me.

Her smile widens and my heart skips a beat, but then my brain reminds me that we're not together and the little flutter I felt is probably anxiousness because of the situation I'm in. Elle motions for me to follow her down the hall. She turns into my office and waits for me before closing the door.

"I didn't expect you to come back."

"Yeah, I figured. I almost didn't, but I'd gone out to my parents to see them."

*I knew it.*

"I should've asked you first if it was okay to tell them about what's going on." Elle wrings her hands together. I should let her know it's okay, but I sort of like watching her squirm. She's usually so confident, I feel like right now, she's second-guessing herself and I can see the remorse in her eyes. "I told them. I'm sorry. I know I should've asked—"

"Elle," I finally stop her. "I had a feeling you were going to go see your parents."

"You did?"

"Yes," I say with some laughter. "I know you better than you know yourself. I also knew you'd tell them, and honestly, I'm glad you did because I don't know if I could look at your parents and tell them what's going on. They've always treated me like family."

"Which brings me to the next thing I have to say."

"Should I be worried?"

Elle eyes me, and I'm officially scared. "Mom says she will be by, which means she's going to bring the entire grocery store with her."

I glance toward the door and think about Katelyn walking in and seeing the mess my family has made. "I made a request for someone to come out and clean. Hopefully they get here tomorrow. At least my mom and Brad are cleaning."

Elle nods. "Another thing. I know you have your oncologist, but I was doing some research—"

"Why?" I interrupt her.

"Why? Because you deserve the best."

"The doctor I have is approved by my insurance," I tell her.

"I don't care about your insurance if he's not the best. I have the money—"

"Elle, you can't buy a cure or pay to make this go away. I have cancer. I have to let science do its thing."

She sighs and sits down at my desk. "Quinn said I shouldn't try and pay for things. I can't help it. I want you to have the best of the best and sometimes it takes money. What if your surgeon . . ." Elle picks up the pamphlet about sperm harvesting off my desk. "Ben, what's this?"

I shake my head. "It's nothing."

"Did you do this?"

"No."

"Are you going to?"

"Nah," I say, shaking my head again. "I don't think so."

"Why not?"

I shrug. "We're not together. I don't see the point."

Elle stands and comes to me. She places her hands on my cheeks and makes me look at her. "Benjamin, I love you. What we're going through is a rough patch." She shows me her ring finger. "I haven't taken my ring off because I believe we have a future."

I step back and her hands drop to her sides. "You didn't take it off because you didn't want your family to know we broke up. It's not because you thought we'd get back together."

"That's not true."

"It's what I believe, and you can't change my mind."

"Fine," she huffs and looks away for a beat. "Your next girlfriend, who could become your wife, will want to have your babies, and you'll want her to have them. Wouldn't you rather have your sperm saved now, instead of regretting things later?"

I go to the window and look out. There isn't much of a view from my office—just our small backyard and the neighboring houses. The view is in the front where our living room, kitchen and bedroom are.

"I'm not going anywhere, Ben," Elle says quietly.

"Until you have to go on a video shoot or leave for a tour or go find your next talent."

"My dad is taking my new band on tour and Uncle Liam is going to help run my office for a bit. Quinn will fill in as well. I'm not leaving your side," she tells me.

"I don't want your pity, Elle. Or your money or the guilt that comes with knowing you're missing work because I'm sick. I'm facing an uphill battle and the last thing I need on my mind is knowing how stressed you are." I can't turn to look at her, out of fear I'll take what I said back and tell her I want her to hold my hand while I go through everything. I do want her there, but I can't just push our problems under the rug.

Elle clears her throat. "I'm not going anywhere, Ben. I'll call this clinic and get you an appointment."

"It's too late."

"What do you mean it's too late? You told me surgery is next week. Surely, they can get you in before . . ." She pauses. "They'll get you in. I'll make sure of it."

I turn and face her. "This is what I'm talking about. I tell you it's too late and you think you can make a phone call and fix everything."

"Be mad at me. I don't care. In five or ten years, when you're married and your wife wants a baby, you can thank me then. Until that happens, Ben, I'm going to do what I can to make sure you have the best of everything. If you think that's pity or I'm doing something I don't want to do, you're wrong." She marches toward me with her finger pointed at my chest. "I love you. You're my best friend, and until December, you were my fiancée. *I. Am. Not. Leaving. You.*"

She wipes away the tears streaming down her face.

"Elle—"

"No, Ben. You don't get to tell me I can't care. That I can't be there for you. That will literally kill me. You're worried about feeling guilty because I'm there, well guess what buddy, you'll feel guilty if I'm not there. My mom, dad, Quinn, they're all going to be there and how is that going to make you feel when I'm not?

"I get that we're not an 'us' anymore, but you know what? We were best friends long before we became lovers, and I want to be there for my best friend."

She covers her face with her hands and sobs. I go to her and pull her into my arms. "Okay, Elle."

"Okay, what?" she mumbles into my chest.

"You win."

She looks up at me. "This isn't a game, Ben. It's life. I want to help you, and this is the only way I know to help."

I study her for a moment and finally give up the fight.

Deep down, I knew once she found out I had cancer, she'd be in takeover mode. I nod and pull her back into my arms. "Please help me."

Elle squeezes her arms around my torso and says, "Of course."

## 13

## ELLE

*B*en invites me to stay for dinner, which he ends up making. He grills salmon, roasts potatoes, and asparagus, while I pick out the wine. He's not supposed to drink, but has a small glass anyway, and tells me it's to calm his nerves. I know they're frayed, and he's on the edge of losing his shit. I would be if I were him. Thankfully, his mother volunteers to clean up after dinner. It seems like Brenda and Brad have seen the light, so to speak, and have realized the potential severity of the situation. Ben's sick. He may look healthy and thriving on the outside, but on the inside, his body is about to wage war against a deadly disease. He shouldn't have to cater to his family. It needs to be the other way around, and if they plan to stay, they're going to need to pitch in. Something needs to be said to them, but the last thing I want to do is upset Ben. He is— and will be—going through enough. He doesn't need me making the situation worse.

After dinner, Ben joins me on the balcony outside our bedroom. Well, I guess it's just his bedroom now. I've always loved the view, and miss being in this house. It's something we found together. It's supposed to be *our* home. He brings me a glass of wine, hands it to me, and then stands to the side. He rests his arms on the railing and sighs.

"It's a beautiful night," he says. "I've always liked it out here at night, just hearing the ocean and not the traffic."

"I know what you mean. I've missed this."

"Where have you been staying?" he asks.

"At the hotel near the studio. Makes things easy."

"What do you want to do about the house?"

*Absolutely nothing.*

"We can talk about that later, after you're cured."

"That could be five years from now, Elle. Do you really want to wait that long to move on from this burden?"

I turn slightly to face him after his statement. He continues to look forward, out into the darkness of the night. If it wasn't for the lights from the surrounding houses, or the glow from the bedroom light, I wouldn't be able to see the expression on his face. He shows zero emotion. No heartache or pain is visible. Ben has closed and locked the door on us and thrown the key into the depths of the Pacific. I don't blame him. I haven't exactly shown him how important he is to me, and when I do or at least try, he can't help but think I'm doing so because he's sick. For the life of me, I can't figure out how to show him otherwise.

"You're not a burden," I tell him, knowing my words fall upon deaf ears. "I'd be here, regardless."

"Really?" He gives me a side-eye glance. "If you were married to someone else, you'd still be here?"

"Yes."

"Don't lie to yourself, Elle. Our relationship, friendship, or whatever we have would be over. There is no way in hell I'm going to hang around and watch you marry someone else or even date another person. As it is, getting over you is going to be hard, especially now."

His words hurt. They stab me in my heart and make me catch my breath. How can he be so mean, and yet stand here next to me so nonchalantly? He didn't have to come outside or bring me wine. Yet, he chose to. Is it because he'd rather wallow in heartache than be with his family? Because to me, it certainly seems like what he's doing.

"You'd give up Quinn?"

Ben shakes his head. "I've already given up family events. I can see Quinn without having to see you or your family."

"I see."

Maybe I shouldn't care about what he's going through and let him battle this on his own, with his freeloading family. Or do one better and demand we sell the house now, instead of waiting. We're definitely not in a split the profit situation, but why should I care?

*I care because I love him.*

I finish my wine and start to walk into the house. Before I cross the threshold, I turn to him and say to his back. "The fertility specialists will harvest your sperm before you go into surgery. We have to be at the hospital at six a.m. The car service will be here at five. Good night, Ben."

He doesn't say anything. His head drops and I hear a slight muttering coming from his mouth, but I don't ask him to repeat himself and say it louder. When I get to the other room, the lights are off as is the television, and Brenda and Brad are nowhere in sight. Makes it easier to make my escape then to have them snicker behind my back.

I'm halfway to the door when Ben's voice rings out. "You're not going back to L.A., are you?"

"Why do you care?" I ask with more bite than intended.

I sigh, shake my head, and continue toward the door. When I reach my car, I hear the front door open and close again.

"Elle?" The way he says my name reminds me of when we're alone, together. The moment before we're about to make love. "You should stay." Ben's hand touches my lower back, and shivers run up and down my spine. I can't help but shake a little at his touch and crave it more.

Turning around, I take him in. The glow of the street-lamp sheds enough light for me to see his eyes. They're red rimmed now, and there's an emotion on his face that was absent when we were on the balcony. My hand cups his cheek. He leans into my touch, moving his head slightly to kiss my palm.

"Don't go."

"I shouldn't stay, Ben. We're not . . ."

"I know and with my family being in the guest bedroom, the options are our bedroom and the couch. I can take the couch if you don't want to share the bed with me."

*I want to share in more ways than you do right now.*

Ben reaches for me, his hand resting on my hip. "I want you to stay. We have an early start in the morning, and I honestly don't know if I'll get in the car if you're not here to push me." He doesn't wait for me to give him an answer. He takes my luggage out of the back of my car and carries it into the house. I follow behind, nervous and sad. I love the idea of sleeping next to him again, but I'm sad because we're not the same anymore.

I'm brushing my teeth when Ben comes into the bath-room. He's wearing a plain T-shirt and a pair of boxers. He's been crying. Seeing him like this tears me up inside. I wish with all my might that I could take away his pain, to ease his suffering. When I finish, I fight the urge to pull him into my arms. He wants there to be a separation between us and I need to honor his wishes, even when it hurts me.

Ben dims the overhead lights as he walks into the bedroom. He crawls into bed and pulls the blankets up to his waist and then rolls onto his side. I make sure the alarm is set on my phone and roll to match him. We lie there, with our hands under our pillows. Neither of us say anything. All our communication is done by the tears that stain our pillowcases.

After what seems like forever, Ben takes my hand in his. "I'm scared," he says into the quiet. "I know you are too. You don't have to tell me. I also know there isn't anything we can do but follow what we're told. The surgeon is going to cut me open tomorrow and remove parts of me. . . I don't know. I can't explain it. I feel like I'm losing my manhood."

"I'm so sorry. I know sorry seems like just a word, but I honestly have no idea what to say."

Ben closes his eyes and snuggles up to our hands. "Thank you for being here."

"Nothing is going to keep me away from you, Ben. Nothing."

❧

SLEEP EVADES US. By the time my alarm goes off, we've moved to the middle of the bed so we're touching, and we held hands all night. Now that we're up, we're moving around the house in silence. Brenda's brewed a pot of coffee and Brad's carried Ben's bag to the doorway. He's currently sitting outside waiting for the car.

"Thanks for the coffee, Brenda."

She nods. "We're going to need it."

"My mom will be by a bit later with breakfast."

106

"And your dad?" she asks. I try not roll my eyes or sigh. I know she has a crush on my dad.

"He's getting ready to take my band on tour, and someone will have to watch Oliver."

"Oliver?"

"Oliver is the foster baby my parents are trying to adopt."

"Wow, isn't your mom old?"

I look at her oddly and shake my head before walking away. In seconds she took something positive and turned it nasty. Regardless of how old my mom is, she and my dad have enough love to spread around to whoever needs it. Besides, my dad is older. But Brenda doesn't care about that.

The car honks when it arrives. I usher Brad and Brenda outside, and slowly coax Ben to the car. He's right, he wouldn't have gone if I hadn't been here. When I go to get in, the back seat is full.

"Mom, go sit in the front, please."

"But Ben."

He shakes his head. "Go or stay here."

Brenda slides out and mutters, "So fucking entitled."

*Yep, I am.* Even when I'm not his girlfriend, Ben prefers me over her. I seriously want to stick my tongue out at her and show her how childish I can be. As soon as Brenda and I are seated, the driver heads toward the hospital.

"Will the press be there?" Brad asks.

"No, why would they be?"

He shrugs.

"I'm not famous," I tell him.

"Still see you guys in the paper sometimes."

"Yeah, I suppose you do. Regardless, we'll take the back

entrance. It's private." My phone lights up with a text from Quinn. I read it and smile. "Quinn's behind us."

Ben turns and looks out the back window. It's still dark and all he can see are the headlights of the car behind. "He didn't have to come."

"He knows that, but you're his friend."

Ben looks out the side window. He rests his elbow on the door and his chin on his fist. He reaches for my hand, and I give it to him freely. Brad huffs but thankfully keeps his comments to himself.

When the driver pulls up to the security booth at the hospital, he rolls the back window down. "Elle James," I give him my name and hope there's some recognition.

"Good morning, Ms. James. What brings you in?"

"Dr. Hilda Rock is expecting us."

"Dr. Rock doesn't open her clinic until nine a.m.," the guard says.

"She's meeting us at six. We're scheduled for surgery at eight," I tell him.

He nods, returns to his booth, looks at his clipboard, and returns. "Mr. James is behind you?"

"Yes," I say, not surprised Quinn arranged to come through this entrance. The guard reaches into his booth and presses the button to raise the bar to let us through to the private garage used mostly by doctors.

"Used your name for this, I see."

"Shut the fuck up, Brad." Ben barks out. "You and mom just need to keep your mouths shut when it comes to Elle and who she is, who her dad is, or how much money she has. Just shut up." I squeeze his hand. He doesn't need this kind of stress ahead of his surgery.

The driver puts the car in park and comes around to Ben's side to open the door. He gets out and keeps ahold of my hand. We wait a few minutes for Quinn to catch up, and as soon as my brother and Ben see each other, they hug. The magnitude of what's about to happen isn't lost on any of us. While Ben's surgery seems routine, surgery is unpredictable.

Quinn says hi to Brenda and Brad, and then pulls me into a hug. "I'm beyond thankful you're here. I don't know if I can handle them by myself," I whisper.

"No worries. Dad is coming later."

I step back and apprise my brother. "Um . . . what about Plum?"

"First stop is Vegas. He'll fly in and fly out. He wants to see Ben." Quinn places his hand on Ben's shoulder.

I nod and motion toward the door. I know we'd all rather shoot the shit in the parking lot, but that won't do Ben any good. He needs to get that tumor out of his body before it does any more damage.

Upstairs, the nurse gets Ben into a room right away, and once he's changed, she tells me I can go in. Except, his mom and brother come with me. I'm annoyed. I also know there isn't anything I can do about it. Only Ben can.

Brenda fluffs Ben's pillows and tucks the blankets in around his legs. Ben absolutely hates having the blankets tucked around him. When she's done, Ben kicks the covers out and I chuckle.

"Good morning," Dr. Rock comes in with a beaming smile.

"I can't thank you enough for doing this, Dr. Rock," I say as she stands at the end of Ben's bed.

"Of course. It's my pleasure to help. I am going to ask everyone to leave the room. This is for Ben's comfort. The procedure itself will only take about ten minutes once we start."

I tell Ben we'll be in the waiting room and leave him with Dr. Rock. In the waiting room, Quinn sits and reads a magazine. When I come in, he puts it down and asks what's wrong. "Nothing, he's in with the fertility specialists."

"For what?" Quinn asks.

"To harvest his sperm," I look at my brother and shrug. "For Ben's future." Ben's, not mine. Not ours.

"I hadn't thought of that."

"Yeah. Ben wasn't going to do it, but I insisted. He may get married someday and she might want to have kids. Now they can." Quinn pulls me to his shoulder for comfort. I'm supposed to be the one Ben marries.

It's an hour later when the nurse lets us know Dr. Rock has left Ben's room and he's asking for me. I go in there, with Brenda left pouting in the waiting room. I knock before entering. Ben's in bed with the covers askew.

"Hey."

"Do you want to know how it went?"

I laugh. "No, I think I have a clear picture of what happens."

"I think I should've read the pamphlet or something. The stuff she showed me . . ."

"The natural way, huh?"

"It was hard to perform, like that," he says, completely mortified.

"Well, it's done."

"Yeah. Listen, I know we didn't talk about this, but I had to sign some papers about what happens to my junk if I die. I gave it all to you and said you or whoever can have kids with it if I die."

I smile softly and run my hand through his hair. "You're not going to die."

"I might."

I shake my head. "Not on my watch," I tell him.

The nurse returns and gives Ben a cap to put on. My heart starts to race, knowing it's almost time for him to go into surgery. When the orderly comes and starts releasing the brakes on Ben's bed, I have to fight back the tears.

"Don't cry," Ben says, quietly.

Nodding. "I love you, Ben."

"Love you, Elle."

Thankfully, I'm allowed to hold Ben's hand until we reach the doors for surgery. He cracks some joke and tells us when we see him again, he'll be ballless. Brad laughs, but Brenda, Quinn and I don't find the humor in it.

Quinn walks me back to the waiting room. Before we round the corner, he tells me he has a surprise for me.

"What is it?"

He points and when my surprise comes into focus, I lose it. My sister rushes toward me, with her arms out wide, waiting to hug me. "Peyton," her name comes out softly. "Oh, God, Peyton, I'm so scared."

"We've got you, Elle. We're here." Her hand strokes my hair. "It's okay," she tells me while I cry into her shoulder. The next thing I know, we're cocooned by Quinn. He's protecting his sisters. Something he's done from the moment we met him.

# 14

# BEN

*W*hen I wake, the quietness in my room is unnerving. Where is everyone? And why does my head hurt? I want to rub my temple but my arm hurts. I adjust slightly and find a tube coming out of my bicep. That's right, I forgot they were going to insert a catheter to make my chemo sessions easier. It's a nice reminder of why I'm here.

Cancer.

I turn my head slightly and see Elle sitting in what looks like an extremely uncomfortable chair, with her eyes closed. I study her for a minute as the sunlight pours into the room and shines on her. She's always been my beacon of light, even when I don't want her to be. She could've given up so easily, and maybe she would've if I didn't have cancer.

In an attempt to clear my throat quietly, I end up waking her. Within seconds, she's at my side, peppering me with questions. Do I need the nurse? Does anything hurt? How do I feel? Elle runs her hand over my hair and smiles at me.

"The doctor said everything went really well."

"Do I still have my balls?"

"Always the jokester," she says. Elle doesn't need to answer my question because I already know the answer. They're gone because they're trying to kill me. "Your scar is pretty small. Not sure it can even be considered a scar."

"So, nothing like Peyton's?"

Elle shakes her head. "Nope, she still beats us all with the gnarly scars." I know Elle's joking. We all hate Peyton's scars, but she's embraced them. I suppose you have to when you've been through what she has.

"Damn, I bet she's going to be pissed."

"No doubt," Elle says. "She's here, along with Noah and Quinn, and your friend John. They're in the waiting room. They've been here the entire time."

"What time is it?"

"A little after seven."

"Damn, I missed dinner. I was really hoping for some of that green Jell-O."

Elle laughs and runs her hand through my hair again. This time her fingers linger on my cheek until she leans in. I expect her to kiss me, to take advantage of my vulnerable state because she knows I won't tell her no, but she rests her head on my chest instead.

"As much as I want to monopolize your time, it'd be unfair of me. Your mom and Brad want to see you. Are you ready for visitors?"

It takes me a minute to nod. I don't really want to see anyone. What I want to do is rollover onto my side and ignore the world—including Elle. Not that she'd let me though. I have a feeling she's going to be up in my face no matter what. She isn't going to take no for an answer, no matter what I say to her.

She leaves the room, and the nurse comes in, followed

by the urologist and oncologist. The doctors go over the next steps in my recovery, although it's not really recovery since I'm going to start chemo and will suffer the side effects. But the good news is, the doctor says they got the entire tumor. I sort of feel like that's his job and if he didn't get the entire thing, he shouldn't be a surgeon. Instead of saying what's on my mind though, I thank him and turn my head to look out the window. I don't want to talk to them anymore. They don't get it, despite them saying "I know what you're going through" or "I know how you feel." Do they really though? Have they been through this or are they just saying what they're taught in medical school?

Empathy sucks.

So does sympathy.

The door to my room opens and the smell of my mother's perfume takes over my senses. I close my eyes and feel her climb onto my bed. I wince when she jostles me, and she instantly starts crying.

"Oh sweetie, I'm so sorry."

*For what?*

"How are you feeling?" Brad asks.

I shrug. I'm pretty drugged up at the moment so the only feelings I have are the thoughts in my brain projecting to my emotions. I'm fucking pissed, and angry, but I don't tell him this. If I were him, I'd start feeling my balls on a daily basis. I know they say cancer isn't hereditary, but what do they know?

Mom insists on sitting on my bed, regardless of how uncomfortable it makes me. "I'm so happy to see you awake."

"Me too," I say because let's be honest, it would suck not to wake up from this.

"I had a chat with Elle while you were in surgery. You really need to create a will, honey."

I close my eyes so she can't see how disgusted I am by her comment. This is not the time, nor place.

"It's unfair that she'd get your portion of your house if something were to happen to you."

"She gets my sperm too," I snap, and her eyes widen. "And she can do whatever she wants with it."

"Benjamin."

"I'm tired." I close my eyes without waiting to see her leave. Except she doesn't. She gets off my bed and turns the television on. Mom channel surfs until she finds Wheel of Fortune. Brad and her start trying to answer the puzzles, while I lie there, trying to heal. What in the fuck is wrong with them? Is this what they consider visiting?

I cough, in a weak attempt to get their attention. When neither of them looks at me, I press the call button for the nurse. Right now, I wish I had to stay in ICU or something where they limit my visitors to one. But nope, general population it is for me.

"What do you need, Ben?" the nurse asks as she comes in. She goes right to my machines, making sure everything is okay. I let my eyes do all the talking and dart them back and forth between her and my family. She nods and tells them she needs to check out my incision and they need to leave the room for a bit.

Brad squeezes my foot when he walks by my bed, but mom peppers me with kisses, telling me how much she loves me. Sometimes I think it's a phrase she says because society tells her it's the right thing to do. I'm not sure she loves anyone except herself. And maybe Brad. She was at least married to his father, while mine just used her—according to her.

"Thank you," I say to the nurse after my family leaves.

"You're welcome. You're our priority, Ben. Anything you need, we're here."

"I appreciate it."

"You do have a waiting room of people though. Your friends are really giving us nurses all the feels."

I chuckle. I can't imagine who she's referring to. "Oh yeah?"

"It seems you're friends with some pretty famous people."

"Ah, yes. I'm a lucky guy."

She rests her hand on my shoulder and laughs. "Or they're lucky to have you."

Elle returns and she has a shit-eating grin on her face. "What did you do?" I ask, knowing full well she's done something. I love her, but she's evil sometimes.

"I sent everyone home.," she tells me. "I figured you'd want some time to rest, and the doctor says you're going to be groggy for a bit. I didn't want you to agree to anything without being fully aware of what you're saying."

She is kind. She is beautiful. But damn, she breaks my heart. "Thank you. Does this mean you're leaving as well?" I don't know how I feel about my question. I want her to stay, but I also don't. Knowing she's here, but not fully here hurts.

"I was planning to sleep in the chair over there. Unless you'd like me to leave. You need your rest, but I know I'm causing you stress right now. It's your choice."

It's not going to matter what I choose. I'll be wrong. I don't want her to go, but I don't want her to stay. I'd love to have things both ways, but I can't.

I nod and say, "You can stay, but under one condition."

"What's that?"

"Well, actually two conditions. No, make that three. I need some Jell-O, preferably green. I also want some real food, so maybe some In-N-Out, and you sleep next to me. I know the bed is small, but I sleep better when you're near me."

"Okay," she says as she sits on the edge of my bed. "I agree to all those conditions."

"Perfect."

"Before I go get dinner and hunt down the Jell-O can we talk about your treatment?"

I shrug, knowing this won't go well.

"I've done some research, and while your oncologist is good, he's not the best."

"He's covered by my insurance," I tell her. "And I like him."

"I get it, and I'm not trying to be pushy, but you deserve to have the best treatment possible and if insurance is in the way, I fear you won't get it."

"I'll be fine, Elle."

Her face falls. I know she wants to be in charge, bark orders, and tell everyone what to do, but this is my battle, and mine alone. I'll take her support, but that's it. I let her convince me on the whole sperm thing, but on treatment, I'm standing firm.

"Okay, Ben." She leans forward and kisses my cheek. "I'll be back. Text me if you think of anything else you need. Love you." She's off my bed and out the door before I can get a response out of my mouth.

THE NEXT MORNING, right after breakfast, there's a knock on the door. "Are you decent?" Quinn's voice rings out. "It's Quinn and Noah."

"Come in," I tell them as I sit up to somewhat greet them. I realize this is the first time I've seen Noah since last year. During that time, he's won the Super Bowl, and because I'm stubborn I missed it.

"Noah, I owe you an apology."

"For what?" he asks.

"For not being there. Holy shit, man. You won the Super Bowl."

He smiles coyly and shakes his head. "My team won. I just threw or passed the ball to some really great players."

"Still. I should've been there."

"Yep, because it won't happen again," Quinn jokes as he slaps Noah's shoulder. The guys pull up two chairs and sit down. "How are you feeling?"

"I'm better. Yesterday was a bit rough, but the doctor says things are looking good. I should be able to go home the day after tomorrow."

"That's great news," Noah says. "Everyone will be so excited."

"Who's out there now?" I ask, motioning toward the wall.

"No one yet," Quinn says. "Elle said she's going to shower and come back. Dad is stopping by later. I believe your mom and Brad are at the house. Mom will be by later. Nola has class this morning and then she's taking Oliver for a bit."

I'm not surprised my family isn't here. They don't do hospitals well, not that anyone does. I look from Noah to Quinn and sense something's up. "Damn, you guys look like you're about to bust my happiness bubble."

"Nah," Noah says, shaking his head. "We're just here to visit and see how you're doing."

"Liars. Spill, what did Elle say to you?"

"Nothing's wrong," Noah says again, this time his voice is a little high-pitched.

"Except we know this isn't true," I tell them. "Let's hear it. I know Elle's mad at me because I won't let her pay for my treatment, so what did she say?"

Quinn clears his throat. "I feel like I need to defend my sister," he starts. "So many people think we've had this easy life when it's not true. The three of us suffer from abandonment issues, even if it doesn't seem like it. It's always in the back of our minds, and sometimes we block our emotions without knowing. Couple this with us growing up the way we did, seeing how hard our dad and uncles work; the three of us forget what should come first, love or work, and sometimes the line is so blurred, we mix them up."

I think I understand what Quinn's saying, but I'm not sure I do.

"Elle loves hard whether it's work or family or you," Noah adds. "She's always been the one to shoulder everything. She gets that from Katelyn after witnessing how she had to be when Mason died. Elle's strong, determined, and like Quinn says her lines between work and love get blurred. But that doesn't mean you're not her priority."

I sigh. "I'm not surprised she's talking about this."

"Nonstop. She's afraid you're going to push her away, which she knows she deserves, but my sister loves you, Ben. I know it may not seem like it, but she does."

"I feel like I love her more than she loves me."

"That's because it took her years to figure it out," Noah says. "Take it from me, loving someone who doesn't—or can't—love you back right away is the worst feeling ever. I feel like Peyton and I lost years because of our age difference."

"Five years isn't a lot," I say to him.

"It's not once the younger one reaches eighteen, but until then, it's bad. Loving Peyton has been one of the hardest and easiest things I have ever done in my life. Deep down I think this is how you see Elle. It's easy to love her, but it's work."

"Like a full-time job," I say, jokingly.

"It's pride," Quinn says. "Sometimes it gets in the way. We want to see ourselves as normal, but we're not. We have busy lives, and the first thing to take a backseat to work is our love lives. Ask Nola. Our relationship looks easy, but that's because she works her schedule around mine. It's unfair of me to ask her to do that, but she does it, and I'm thankful. But someday, she's going to want me to do the same, and it'll be a challenge. But I love her, so I'll do whatever I must to keep her happy, and in turn, she does what she can to keep me happy. Our relationship is a work in progress."

"At least your women aren't bossing you around and telling you that you suck at your job," Noah says with a shake of his head. "Imagine walking into your wife's gorgeous office only to sit and have her tell you where you need to fix your game."

Quinn and I laugh. Noah has a point. He probably has it worse than any of us. Elle was my boss, but she never told me I was wrong about anything I did. We worked well as a team, and I let something as stupid as a date get in the way.

There's a knock on the door and Harrison peaks his head in. "Hey guys."

"Wow, the red carpet has been rolled out for me," I say

as Harrison greets me with a hug. "Liam and JD here as well?"

"Oh God no," Harrison says. "JD and nurses are never a good idea." Harrison shakes his head. "And Liam's in Las Vegas covering for me right now. I told Elle I'd take her new band on tour for her." He doesn't add while she babysits me, not that he would.

Quinn and Noah excuse themselves, and Harrison sits down. "Does the staff know you're eating greasy burgers?" He motions toward the garbage can where Elle hasn't hid the evidence well.

"The hospital food sucks. I don't know how they expect people to get better on crap food. This morning my eggs were so hard I could've given myself a concussion with them."

"Well, it's a good thing Elle's got you covered. How are you doing? Katelyn and I are really sorry you're going through this and want you to know, the doors open. It's always open, Ben. Regardless of what's going on between you and Elle. We consider you to be a part of our family."

"Thank you, that means a lot."

"Honestly, I'm a bit saddened as to why you didn't come to us."

I shrug. "You're Elle's parents. Not mine. I don't want her to think I'm using her."

"Son, you've been hanging around our house from the moment you moved to Beaumont. Not once has it ever crossed our minds that you might be using Elle or Quinn. You are one of the most genuine men I have ever met, and you never gave me a reason to question you nor your integrity. Not then, and definitely not now."

Harrison's words stab me right in the heart. A couple

tears fall before I wipe them away. To me, he's always been the father I never had, and I've always looked up to him.

"I broke up with her." My voice cracks. "At the time, I thought it was the right thing to do because I want to get married, and she wants to wait until everyone's schedules are clear. I feel like she pushed my needs aside and when I asked her to elope, she got mad at me because she wants you to walk her down the aisle, which I'll be honest, I'm not sure I understand."

"I get it," Harrison says. "You see things differently than she does. She was raised by a calendar, everything we did and continue to do, depends on others and when events are booked years in advance, asking for a change is hard. I think we could've worked something out, but she's never asked before. It's always been a 'put it on the calendar and if I can be there, I'll be there' type of thing. While the kids were growing up, I missed my fair share of events, but the one thing I will *not* miss is their weddings and the birth of my grandchildren. Elle knows this, and I think in the back of her mind, she feels she needs to wait until the tours are over. She's trying to juggle being a manager, a daughter, and a fiancée. But her most important job has always been as your friend. You've been friends longer than you've been a couple. You know she has a good heart and would never do anything to hurt you."

"Deep down, I think I know this. I'm just mad."

"At her?"

I nod. "And the world."

"It's not fair to compare her to the world. She's only one person."

"I know. I'm also jealous. She spends so much time with the bands."

"And up until Christmas, I thought you were as well.

Working together, especially in this business, it's the best thing for couples. You're together. You're bonding and building, both personally and professionally. Why'd you quit?"

I shrug. "I was mad at her for choosing Christmas over me. I regretted it instantly but asking her for my job back seemed like a bad idea. Nothing would've been fixed between us, and I have a hard time seeing her and not being with her."

Harrison chuckles. "I get it. I was there once with Katelyn."

It hits me in this moment that I haven't met Oliver yet. "Congratulations, by the way," I tell him. "Can you let Mrs. KPJ know that it's pretty awesome you guys are trying to adopt Oliver. I hope to meet him soon."

Harrison smiles. "I'll let her know. I'll be honest, I thought I was done with kids until one of them decides to bless us with grandbabies, but having this little guy around makes me realize how much I've missed having a baby around."

"I'm sure Peyton and Noah are trying to make you and Liam grandpas."

Harrison bends over with laughter. "Liam will lose his mind. He's forever young. Look, I didn't come here to talk about Elle or make excuses for her. I came to see you and to let you know, you're not alone. This isn't a fight you're going to manage by yourself. I'm here. Katelyn's here. We're a family and we stick together. Katelyn fully expects your treatment schedule so she can sit with you while you get your chemo. She already started making a list of things you're going to do together while you're sitting there. I should warn you though, she's dabbling in screenplay writing and I fear you might be her next

123

victim." Harrison cringes. "I mean her next test subject."
He laughs.

After our laughter dies down, I look at Harrison and say,
"Thank you."

"For what?"

"For showing me how to see things differently, especially when it comes to Elle. I sometimes forget not everything is black and white with her, and need a reminder," I
pause and take a deep breath. "Especially before it's too
late."

## 15

### ELLE

*I*t's been twenty-one days since Ben's surgery, not that I'm counting or anything. The physical parts of Ben have healed, but the emotional scars, I fear will be there forever. At night, I often hear him crying in the shower, when he thinks no one can hear him. I want to comfort him, but I don't know how. I don't know what it's like to lose a part of you in the way he has. Since his surgery, he's gone to therapy, and the therapist suggested testicular prosthesis as it could help with Ben's psychological fears of inadequacy. Of course, when he's confiding in me about this, his brother overhears and thinks it's some sort of joke, and teases Ben about getting fake balls. I hate Brad. He makes me angry to the point of tears, but I can't do anything about it. He's here and, besides their mom, he's Ben's only family. As much as I want to tell him and Brenda to pound sand and get the hell out, I don't. Deep down, I think they mean well, they just don't know how to show it because they've never been a close family.

In the past three weeks, I've been back at work, trying to get Sinful Distraction's marketing plan done for their new single, getting Talking Til Dawn into the studio, and having daily video conference calls with my dad and Plum. Plum is having the time of their lives, and their tour has been extended by two more weeks. Thankfully, my dad isn't complaining, and Plum isn't either. I've shared their numbers with them, and their song is slowly creeping to the top of the charts. Still, I feel like I owe it to them to be the best manager possible, but I don't want to leave Ben. I guess I finally understand what Maverick meant when he said he wasn't leaving his wingman even though the prize was right in front of him. Except, Ben's my prize.

Our friendship is back on track. We still share a bed, but we did this while being friends. Each morning, I wake up on his chest, which was something we didn't do as friends, but he doesn't seem to mind. I suppose after today, our sleeping habits will have to adjust. I've read every possible article I can find about chemotherapy and radiation, and the side effects. Ben's going to be tired, he's going to bruise easily, he's going to be sick, and he's going to lose his hair. I haven't broached the subject about his hair with him, but I know he's concerned. Honestly, I fully expect the guys to band together and have a shave party. I can see my brother and Noah organizing something like this, and I think Brad would do it as well. He keeps his hair pretty short to begin with.

I leave the office and head toward the house in Malibu. I needed some time to myself this morning, and work is my escape. It's the one place where no one judges me for wanting to work. Last week, I opened my laptop in the kitchen while Ben cooked—it was his idea, not mine—because I wanted his opinion on a couple of bands, and Brenda lost her shit, going on and on about how her boy is sick and all I care about are the demos in my inbox. I don't know what she expects me to do. Yes, he has cancer, but we were in this limbo stage between surgery and chemo. He had to heal. And he needs to feel human again. If making dinner and talking about music makes him feel like himself again, I want to encourage him.

By the time I arrive home, my somewhat good mood is in the dumps. Living in this house is awkward and uncomfortable, with Brenda hovering and Brad milking us dry. The only reprieve I get is at night, when it's just Ben and me, in our room. Often, we lie on our sides and just look at each other, letting our souls do all the talking. He's hurting and I hurt for him.

Inside, Brad's on the couch, thankfully with clothes on, and playing a video game. I swear, someday he's going to find the console missing. He doesn't say anything when I walk past, which is shocking because it's usually shit like, "the bathroom is out of toilet paper" or "there aren't any dishes." I'm a convenience to him because if I'm here, he knows Ben will be taken care of, which in turn, takes care of Brad.

I look all over the house for Ben but can't find him. I'm frustrated because he didn't text me that he was leaving and now I have to ask his brother where he went. "Do you know where Ben is?"

Brad never takes his eyes off the television and mutters, "Beach."

Perfect, the same place I go to when I need peace and quiet. I head outside and toward the beach. As soon as my feet touch the sand, I slip my shoes off and trudge toward the shore. Surfers and swimmers clutter the water, while umbrellas, blankets, towels, and those popular sun tents take up most of the sandy beach space.

It takes me a few minutes, but I find Ben, sitting in the

sand with his ankle strap still secured and his board next to him. I sit down and pull my knees to my chest. "Did you surf?"

"Thought about it."

I don't bother telling him he's not supposed to do any strenuous activities for another three weeks, and he has to be cleared by the urologist first. He doesn't need a lecture. He needs a friend. "Water looks choppy."

"I figured today would be my last day to surf."

"The surgeon will clear you in three weeks. You'll be good to go."

"I'll be sick."

"I know." I sigh. Ben knows the chemo and radiation are going to wreck his body. He's going to be weak, tired, and unwilling to eat because everything will taste gross or not have any flavor at all.

He's going to be sick. He's going to puke his guts out, and then puke some more. He's going to bruise easily, need blood transfusions, and we have to monitor who is around him. If they're sick, they can't come near him. Brad and Brenda don't know this, but while we're at chemo today, I have a service coming in and cleaning the house from top to bottom. There will be new rules in place, and if they don't like them . . . well I won't be sad to see them leave. Unfortunately, Brenda's current lack of a job and housing puts me in a tough spot, and I'd have to put her up somewhere, but Brad can go back to his place, and his garage. He has a viable job and a garage to run. I understand his brother is going through a life-changing event, but his moody outlook isn't needed. Ben needs to be surrounded by light and positivity. I want him to see the future and feel like he has more than a fighting chance. Brad parked on our couch isn't doing Ben any favors.

"I guess it's time to go, huh?"

"Yeah," I say, sadly. I don't want him to have to go through this any more than he wants to. Ben stands and reaches for my hand to help me up, and then his board. I expect him to let go of me, but he doesn't. Together, we walk back to the house, and I wait for him while he stores his board on the rack. "Do you want to take a shower before we go?"

He shakes his head. "The smell of sun and sand comforts me."

"Me too," I tell him.

On the drive over, we listen to the radio. Plum's song, "Last Day," comes on and I can't help but smile and turn the volume dial up. My head starts bobbing while my finger taps the steering wheel. When it's over, my smile turns into the biggest grin possible when the DJ talks about the girls and how they're the next big thing.

"Is that your new band?" Ben asks.

"One of them, yes. They call themselves Plum. I wasn't sold on the name at first, but it's grown on me and now I love it."

"That was a really great song."

"Justine wrote it. I have an acoustic version up on the streaming sites. She's a brilliant songwriter. Quinn really enjoys working with her, as well as Wynonna and Priscilla, who are sisters."

"I'd say they have to be with names like that."

"What do you do for them?" Brad asks.

"As their manager, I make sure they're in the studio and working with the best producers. I manage their day-to-day. I fight for them when it comes to the labels. I get them the airtime I think they deserve. Set up tours. That sort of thing."

"So, you boss them around and take their money."

I glance in my rearview mirror and throw daggers at Brad. Unfortunately, he's looking out the window and doesn't see me.

"Brad, cut the shit," Ben says. "Seriously, just fucking stop."

"It's okay, Ben," I say quietly.

"No, it's not," he fires back.

"I'm just trying to figure out what she does," Brad says in lame defense of his comment.

"What she does is protect artists from fucking vultures. Kind of like shitty mechanics taking advantage of their customers."

"Fuck you," Brad spits out.

Ben shakes his head. I rest my hand on his leg and give it a squeeze. I wish he'd tell his brother to leave. I know it's unfair of me to feel this way because Ben needs his family around him, but I can't help it.

"You boys need to stop," Brenda says. It's the wisest thing she's said since I've known her.

I pull into the private entrance of the hospital and give the guard my name. After we park, we head to the cancer wing and Ben checks in. Within seconds, a nurse comes out to get him. He clutches my hand when his name's called.

"Hi Ben, I'm Hope and I'm going to be your nurse today."

Brad scoffs and I give him a pointed look. "Nice to meet you. This is my . . ." Ben looks at me and I smile. I don't care what he calls me at this point, and while I prefer he call me his fiancé, I'm not going to force him. "My Elle," he finally says, which makes my heart soar. "My mom, Brenda, and the jerk over there is my brother, Brad. Feel free to ban him if he gets on your nerves."

Hope laughs and tells Ben to follow her. I pull him into my arms and tell him I'll be right here when he's done. He lingers for a moment and finally follows Hope behind the double doors. Once he's out of sight, I turn to Brenda and Brad. I open my mouth to say something, but then think better of it. I don't want to fight with them, especially not here. More so, because I don't want either of them to say stupid shit to Ben. He has enough to deal with.

I sit down and pull my laptop out. I'm not leaving the lounge until Ben's ready to go home. I want to be inside with him, holding his hand and keeping him company, but all the money in the world can't circumvent some policies. It's dangerous for anyone to be in there, not receiving treatment. The drugs they're pumping into patients are harmful, even more so to the people who aren't battling cancer. I have to remember this is where we have to be in order for Ben to get better.

# BEN

*I*t's been two weeks and I already want to give up. My house is sterile, and it feels weird to be there. I know why Elle did what she did, but I hate being home. There's a live in . . . well, I don't know what to call him. He cleans up after me. It doesn't matter what I do, he's behind me. If I go to the bathroom, he comes in right after me and cleans the toilet. If I change my clothes, he washes my other ones immediately. I know it's to protect me from these fucking drugs running through my system, but I feel like a freak, and I hate it.

This is my off week. My week to rest and rejuvenate if that's even possible. I don't want to leave the house, and I don't want anyone here. Except for Elle. She seems to be the only one to understand I need space. She works in the office, while I sit on our balcony and stare at the water, wondering how long it would take to swallow me whole. Elle checks on me for food or if I want some company, and then goes back to work. Honestly, I think she's writing a book or streaming shows on her laptop because I don't know how she's getting any work done. She should be out scouting for talent and signing new artists, but she's here, by my side. At first, I thought of her as a babysitter, but she's more than that. She's my voice when I feel like I don't have one, and as much as I hate to admit it, I need her. Yet, I feel like I have nothing to offer her.

There's a small knock behind me and I turn my head slightly, but not enough to see who it is. I know it's Elle by the lightness in the way she tapped her knuckles against the glass. She takes the seat next to me and sighs. The sun is starting to take a bit longer to set these days. Back when I chased after Elle, this was my favorite time of the year, when the sun would stay out as long as possible. I always felt like once I went to sleep, my quest to make her mine would have to start all over again, like that movie *50 First Dates* with Adam Sandler and Drew Barrymore. Adam's character, Henry, was in love with Drew's character Lucy, only she had a traumatic brain injury and her memory reset every day. Each day, Henry would reintroduce himself to Lucy and try to win her over. That's how I felt about Elle. Each day was a new challenge, and once she realized she was in love with me, I never wanted to let her go.

I reach for her hand and intertwine our fingers together. I love her but haven't told her in a while. Those words don't seem to hold the weight they used to or maybe it's vice versa. Now, if I tell her, it'll be because I feel like I'm dying. I'm not as optimistic as she is. I can't manifest happiness. Right now, everything is gloom. My world is gray. It's bleak. I know I'll get worse before I get better, but I don't know how much more I can take. My body hurts. I've lost weight, my hair is falling out, I can't eat because food is disgusting, and when I shower, I can't help but touch the part of me that's missing. My sack is empty and that makes me feel meaningless, like I'm no longer a man.

"Do you want to go for a walk?"

I shake my head. "I'm not feeling very well," I tell her. This isn't an excuse, but fact. I feel warm, but I'm freezing. It's eighty out and I should be sweating, but my teeth chatter instead.

"Is everything okay . . . besides the obvious?" I huff at the last part of her statement. She started adding this after I vomited my guts out for the first time. Of course, her handy dandy cleaner was right behind me, sterilizing the bathroom.

"I don't know. I feel off."

"What can I do to help?" she asks, but I just shake my head. "Ice cream? There's a pint of Ben & Jerry's in the freezer with our names on it."

"What kind?"

"Chocolate chip cookie dough."

"Okay." The sound of ice cream actually sounds good right now, even though I'm cold. Elle tells me she'll be right back and when she returns, she has two bowls in her hands and gives me one of them. Before cancer, we'd share the pint, but now I have to be careful about bodily fluids. Before cancer, we'd eat the entire pint in one sitting, but now I get a scoop. If I finish it, I'll be happy.

"Did you know Ben & Jerry's came out with cookie dough bites? You can get them in the freezer section of the store. They make for a great snack on a road trip or something to have around the house when you want something sweet, but don't want to bake cookies."

"When's the last time you baked cookies?"

Elle laughs. "Christmas, I guess."

"Sorry I wasn't there."

"It's okay. Maybe we'll go back this year."

"It's not okay, Elle. None of this is okay. I don't know why you're even here. I wouldn't be if I were you."

"Where's all of this coming from, Ben?"

I set my barely eaten ice cream onto the table between us. "I treated you like shit, and you're here, taking care of me. I've said some really mean things to you, and yet you never gave up."

"Ben?"

"I'm dying, Elle. I can feel it. I'm supposed to remain positive and have a sunny outlook about this situation, but I don't. I picture the cancer ravishing my body and taking over like the parasite it is. I can't stop thinking the worst is going to happen. I can't help but think that if I had gone on the trip to Vermont, none of this would've happened to me."

"You think this is some type of karma?" she asks.

I nod. "If I wasn't so selfish and demanding—"

"You stop that right now, Benjamin Miller. This pity party for one doesn't have a reservation. You didn't get cancer because of karma or because you didn't go on the Christmas trip. You got cancer because of who knows what. Not because you didn't take a trip or because you called off our wedding. You were right to do that, Ben. I was putting my career before everything. My desire to build a successful business and the fear of letting people down blinded me from what was most important—you. I'm not going to make that mistake ever again."

Elle stands in front of me and cups my cheeks. "You're the love of my life, Ben. My best friend, my perfect companion. You are my sun. My moon. My everything. I am right where I want to be."

"You want to care for an invalid?"

"You're far from an invalid, Ben. You're sick and your

135

treatment drains any energy you have. Once it's done, you'll be the same Ben as you were before."

"Minus—"

"Yes, I know, minus your balls." She rolls her eyes and grins.

The way she says it makes me laugh. I know I harp on not having them, but when you're used to them being there, you notice these things. Knowing the way I feel, I can't imagine how a breast cancer survivor feels.

"I love you, Ben. I hope you know this here." She places her hand on my heart. "I am right where I want to be. We're in this battle together."

"I love you too."

"Good, now let's talk about the negative outlook you have." Elle doesn't chastise me for the outlook I have but makes me promise to try and change the way I see things, especially in my mind. Instead, she wants me to play Star Wars or whatever game I want with the tumor and pretend to battle it. I know she means well, but she's never seen a single Star Wars movie and has no idea what she's talking about. Still, she's cute for trying.

It's the middle of the night when I reach for her. "Elle."

"What is it?" she asks, her voice groggy with sleep. We share a bed, but not blankets, and I sleep on a mattress pad. Something that can be thrown out if it gets soiled.

"Something's wrong."

She turns the bedside lamp on and looks at me. "Where?"

"Inside. I don't know, I can't explain it. Something's not right. I hurt all over and I have a fever."

"Okay," she's out of bed and on her phone before I realize she's called for an ambulance. It's probably safer this way, instead of driving in the middle of the night, plus I can get medical attention much faster. "The ambulance is on its way. Do you want to get dressed?"

Elle helps me sit up, but it's as far as I make it. Every muscle in my body hurts to move and I'm too weak to stand up. Red lights flash outside, and Elle goes to meet the crew. I can hear my mother yelling, acting as if I'm mortally injured. Her wailing is a nuisance. She beats the paramedic into the bedroom and all but throws herself at me.

"Mom, stop." She bumps into my arm where my port is, and I cry out.

"Excuse me, ma'am," the medic says as he assesses my vitals. He asks me questions, checks the dressing over my port, and finally helps me stand. I buckle against him, but he holds me upright. He's strong, where I am weak.

Elle's by my side, dressed and with a duffel bag thrown over her shoulder. "Going somewhere?" I ask her, weakly.

"I'm going with you," she tells me.

"I'm coming too. So's Brad," my mom says.

"No, just Elle. I only want her." Thankfully, I can't see my mom's expression, but I can see Elle's. She's grateful. I reach for her hand, and she gives hers freely until it's time to move me to the ambulance. "Can she ride with me?"

"Of course," the medic says, as he straps me to the stretcher.

Once I'm inside, Elle climbs in and sits next to the medic. This tin box is equipped with everything, and if I wasn't strapped to the bed, I'd push and pull on every gadget all while saying, "what's this do?" Surely, I'd get my hand slapped.

The lights stay on, but thankfully there isn't a siren.

This means I'm not dying. Just really fucking sick. The medic hooks me up to a couple of machines, and they start beeping. Believe it or not, the sound is soothing, and I close my eyes.

I jostle awake and find Elle standing outside of the ambulance. She walks next to me, with her bag slung over her shoulder and stays with me until I'm put into a room. Two nurses come in and one asks me a couple of questions, while another one draws my blood and hooks me up to a bag of saline. When they leave, Elle comes into the room.

"I hate this place."

"I don't believe anyone is a fan of hospitals, Ben."

"Except for the people who work here."

"This is true."

After what feels like an hour, and after I've had some X-rays, the on-call doctor stops by to visit. "Hey Ben, I'm Dr. Wilder. I looked over your blood work and it looks like you've got an infection in your intestines. We're going to keep you here for a bit and give you some fluids and antibiotics and see how you respond."

"Does this mean the cancer has spread?" I ask him.

"Not at all. Just means there's a pesky germ out there and you caught it. You'll be good to go in no time." While he's talking, the nurse comes in and adds a bag to my IV, and just like that, they start mending me. Before Dr. Wilder can leave, an orderly comes and moves us to a private room. It's nice and dark, but the blinds are open and from this floor, there's a beautiful view of the city.

Elle goes to close the curtains, but I tell her to leave them open. "Come lie with me."

She does as I ask and makes sure there's an extra layer of blanket between us. The last thing I want to do is expose her to the chemo drugs.

We lie there, looking out the window.

"From here, the city looks peaceful."

"That's because most people are sleeping," she says.

"You should go back home."

She shakes her head. "I'm not leaving your side."

I hug her a little tighter. "You'd rather be here than with my mother. I can't say I don't blame you. She really needs to go."

"It's your call."

"Brad and her talk about money all the time. I think they're going to ask you for a loan." Elle stiffens in my arms. "If either of them does, you tell them no. Don't give them a single cent. Promise me."

"I promise."

"I want to go home, Elle."

"I know, Ben. You won't be here long."

"No, I want to go back to Beaumont. I want to be away from the city, and just be home."

Elle sits up and looks at me. "What are you saying?"

I play with a long strand of her hair. "Will you take me back to Beaumont?"

She nods. "Of course. I'll arrange for everything."

# 17

# ELLE

*J*n the morning, while Ben waits for his discharge papers, his oncologist comes in and discusses moving his treatment to Beaumont. It's not ideal, but Ben wants to be there, and frankly, so do I. I like the idea of being where no one cares who I am, or who my parents are. Where we can walk the streets, go to the park, and eat out without someone shoving a camera in our faces or asking about my family. The people in Beaumont are different. They don't care about the fact Liam Page lives there or that they'll find him drinking coffee in Whimsicality. To them, he's Liam Westbury, local teen hero turned family man. He's the one they count on to volunteer or organize a fundraiser for a family in need.

"Here's what we can do," Dr. Dowling says. "I'll fly out to Beaumont every third week for a checkup, and we'll run your scans at that time, check your progress, everything you would've done here. I'll conference with the staff at Beaumont General and let them know what we're doing with our aggressive treatment plan. I'll also make sure they have my cell phone number for any emergencies. Any changes to your treatment will have to be approved by me as well."

"Thank you, Dr. Dowling" Ben says. "I know this is a big inconvenience for you, but I need to get out of town, and away from this place."

"I wish I could say I understand, but I don't," he says as he stands and shakes his head. "I'll see you in a couple of weeks."

I give Ben a reassuring squeeze on his shoulder and when the door closes, he looks at me. "Am I making a mistake?"

"I don't believe so, but if we get to Beaumont and it's not working, we'll come back. It's as easy as that. Besides, this will work. I think you'll be happier, and we have friends there."

"I don't want to hang out with anyone outside of our family." He meets my gaze and I smile at him softly. I love that he's finally saying "our" family instead of "your" family. I've told him repeatedly, throughout so many years, my family is his. My parents have said it as well. It's time he starts recognizing this.

It takes the nursing staff a couple of hours to get Ben's discharge papers ready to go. Of course, he has to have a couple more tests, and we have to wait for the lab to read the results before the nurses even begin to start the process.

"Did you call your grandpa?"

"I did. He's excited for us to come visit."

"I still can't believe he lives in that big house by himself."

"I know. I thought for sure he would've moved to be near us or at least moved to a condo. Mom has offered many times, but he always says no. I worry about him being alone."

"Doesn't Josie check on him every day?"

I nod. "Or Liam. Mom says Mack has been going over, mowing the lawn, and helping Liam with maintenance on the house."

"Mack, really?" Ben looks confused and it dawns on me that he has no idea about Nick and Aubrey. My hand hits my forehead and I feel my eyes go wide.

"I forgot to tell you!" I sit down at the end of his bed, and Ben moves into a cross-legged position. "So, Mack shows up at Christmas, which is when we find out that Nick and Aubrey are getting divorced and she's going back to South Africa. She took Amelie with her and Mack was supposed to stay in Beaumont with Nick. Except, Nick went to Cape Town to make sure Aubrey found a place in a safe neighborhood and hasn't come back yet. Believe me, it was a total shocker when Mack walked in."

"Wow, I guess I missed a lot at Christmas."

"Eh, you missed drama, which I guess you get with any big family function."

"I missed meeting Oliver."

I nod. "Yeah, but we can arrange a meeting when your chemo treatments are done."

"You know, I never opened the presents you left at the house."

"Where are they?"

"In the closet in the downstairs basement."

"Where Brad's sleeping?"

Ben nods and his eyes widen. I have a feeling he's thinking the same thing I am. They've become Brad's presents. Brad isn't a bad guy, he's just a guy who can't help himself sometimes.

"Wanna take a wager on if they're still there or not?" I joke.

Ben shakes his head. "Nope. I forgot all about them until now, but I should probably thank your parents for whatever they bought me."

"Mom knows you're thankful, Ben."

"Still."

I nod and smile softly. I don't want to argue with him.

Finally, the nurse returns with Ben's discharge papers. She reminds him to call or come in if his fever spikes or if he's feeling any soreness in his arm, where his port is.

In the car, Ben stares out the window. We're in traffic and moving at a snail's pace. "What's on your mind?"

"I feel bad."

"About?"

"About asking you to take me to Beaumont after I fought with you about my care. Surely, this is the place to be."

I reach across the console to hold his hand. "If Beaumont is where you need to be to heal, so be it. I talked to my dad, he'll make sure the jet is available to fly the doctor in and out, and I'm confident the staff at Beaumont General can handle your case."

"But they're not the best."

"No, they're not, but we can bring the best to you. I'm not going to let anything happen to you, Ben."

When we get home, I follow Ben into the house. When he gets to the top of the stairs that lead to the main floor of our home, he pauses. I sidestep around him and do the same thing. Our once spotless house is a complete and utter pigsty and there's a woman straddling Brad.

"What in the fuck is going on?" Ben barks out. The woman startles, launches herself off Brad's lap and tries to cover her chest before Ben and I get an eyeful. I feel bad for her. I bet she has no idea this isn't Brad's house.

"You're back early," Brad says meekly.

"We sit on that couch, Brad."

He looks at the leather and shrugs. "It's not like you and Elle don't do shit on it."

"It's our Goddamn couch. We can do whatever the hell we want on it!" Ben replies tersely.

"What's all this yelling?" Brenda asks as she comes up the stairs behind us. She doesn't greet Ben or ask how he's doing. She didn't even come see him at the hospital even though Quinn offered to give her a ride when he picked up my car. The dramatic shit she pulled the night before was just for show.

"This . . ." Ben spreads his arms out. "Are you guys kidding me with this shit?"

"What?" Brenda asks as she shrugs. "It's not like you don't have a housekeeper."

"That's not how it works, Mom!" Ben pushes his hand over the hat he's wearing. He's taken to wearing one since he starting chemo in preparation for his falling out.

"Well, why not? Why shouldn't we live in the lap of luxury? Why should we have to clean up and do housework when she can afford to pay for someone else to do it?" Brenda crosses her arms over her chest and waits for Ben to answer her. As much as I want to say something, I don't. I can't. It's not my fight. Ben needs his family and I'll bite my tongue to keep the peace.

"You're right," he says, looking at me.

"I am?" I ask and he nods.

He turns to his mom and shakes his head. "I want you gone. You too, Brad. You're stressing me out and I don't need the stress. I'm fucking sick and you think it's okay to live like pigs."

144

"Ben, you don't mean that. It's Elle putting thoughts into your head."

I scoff but say nothing.

"No, it's me realizing Elle's been right the entire time. You're so obsessed with her money and status you're willing to use me to get to her. I don't want you here. I want you both gone, now."

"Benjamin—"

"Stop!" He holds his hand up to interrupt his mom. "Go to Brad's. He has a place and a job, unless the bank has foreclosed on it, and if they have, don't come running back to me. I can't deal with your shit when I'm trying to deal with my own."

Ben takes my hand and leads us down the hall to our bedroom. He closes the door after I step in and locks it.

"I'm sorry."

"Don't be," he says. "I thought with me having cancer, she'd actually step up and be a mother instead of whatever the hell she is."

"I know. But I'm still sorry. You shouldn't have to deal with this. Not now. Not ever."

Ben smiles, but it doesn't reach his eyes. "We should pack."

We go into the closet, but I continue to the bathroom and bring the stool from my vanity back with me so Ben can sit when he needs to rest. I'm thankful I made the decision to move back in. I think Ben was happy as well . . . at least until all my clothes came back.

❧

BEN SLEEPS the entire way to Beaumont and startles when the plane touches down. He looks out the window and smirks. "It's like night and day compared to where we live. Where are all the planes? The lights? The noise?"

"We left it all behind."

"Yeah," he says as he sighs. When the plane stops, we unbuckle, and I help him stand. He's tired. I thought the blood transfusion and antibiotics would give him some energy, but they haven't. He's only two weeks into his chemo and he's exhausted all the time. I honestly didn't expect it to be like this.

The door opens and before we even take a step, Liam is on the plane, walking toward us. I want to jump into his arms and ask him to take away my pain, but he's not here for me. He's here for Ben.

"Hey," he says when he sees us. "We're glad you're here."

"Us too. Thank you for coming to get us," I say as we hug. "I really appreciate it."

"Hey, Ben."

"Hey, Liam. Did you roll the red carpet out?" Ben and Liam laugh.

"I thought about it. You guys haven't been back since Peyton and Noah's wedding. We've missed you around here." Liam points down the aisle. "Let's get you off the plane. Josie's in the car, waiting,"

I go first with Ben in the middle and Liam bringing up the rear. I can see it in Liam's eyes, he wants to assist Ben, but he also doesn't want to emasculate him either. It's hard to help without making someone feel weaker than they are.

Outside, Josie stands next to their SUV while someone from the airport loads our luggage into the back of their car. Tomorrow, after things have settled down, I'll rent a car. My grandpa will tell me to use his, but I don't want to leave him without one.

I hug my aunt and cry into her shoulder. She squeezes me tightly and tells me everything is going to be okay. "We're not going to let anything happen to him."

"I'm so scared."

"You've got us to lean on. Come on, your grandpa is waiting for you."

The thought of seeing my grandpa brings a smile to my face. Josie insists that Ben sit in the front. She climbs into the back with me. Liam drives us through town and down Main Street. I have to do a double take when I see all the changes our little town has gone through.

"Did someone buy the buildings around Whimsicality?" I ask my aunt.

"Yep, someone did," Liam says. I glance at the rearview mirror and see him smiling. "We bought it and have slowly been renovating. We rent out the spaces to others, giving them a chance to follow their dream of owning a business, but without the maintenance. I opened a recording studio on the second floor. There's also a dentist office, a dance studio, and a photography studio. We renovated one space into an apartment."

"How come you didn't tell us this at Christmas?"

"Your parents know," Josie says. "You'll have to ask your mom why she didn't tell you."

"Wow. I can't believe she's keeping these secrets. Wait, we have a bookstore now?"

Liam laughs. "Beaumont's growing. We even have a Dunkin'. That one we fought because of Whimsicality, but we haven't seen a decline in business. The true Beaumonters prefer our coffee, while the transplants take the other stuff."

"I guess the secret's out," Ben says. "We all knew this place was magic."

After we pull into my grandpa's driveway, I lean forward and look out the window. I expect to see him on the porch, rocking in the swing, but it doesn't even look like he's home.

"Uncle Liam," I say after we both get out of the car. "I want to thank you and Mack for helping my grandpa. I know he's not your responsibility. I've tried to convince him to move to California. If you want, we can hire people to take care of things. I already changed the housekeeper to be here every day while we're here."

Liam puts his hands on my shoulders. "Elle, you never ever have to thank me for taking care of Michael. He's like a father to me. There isn't anything I wouldn't do for him."

I nod my thanks and then wrap my arms around his waist. After I release him, he rushes over to the passenger side and makes sure Ben has an easy time getting out of the car. Josie leads the way up the walkway and the stairs and waits for us to join her before opening the door. She holds the screen while I go in.

"Well, it's about time you got here," Peyton says as she walks toward us with Oliver on her hip.

"What are you guys doing here?" I take the baby from her and give him kisses. Peyton doesn't answer me as she goes to Ben and gives him a hug.

"Ben?" I get his attention and then look at Oliver. "This is Oliver." Ben comes forward and waves. "Oliver, this is your Uncle Ben. Can you say Ben?" Oliver squeals.

"He's a happy baby," Ben says.

"Very happy."

"Is Mom here?" I ask Peyton.

"Yep, but she's at the store. Noah's with Mack and Betty Paige. We didn't want to overwhelm Ben."

"Where's Grandpa?

"With Mom."

"Do you think you could hang with Ben for a bit? He's good on meds and all that. He doesn't need any help or anything. He just needs to rest."

"Where are you going?"

"I need to go visit our father and I want to do it now before everyone gets here."

Peyton nods and takes Oliver from me. I tell Ben where I'm going and how long I'll be. He settles himself on the couch and Liam sits down next to him. They start talking about baseball and I know that's my cue to duck out. Peyton gives me the keys to her car, and I drive a bit faster than I should to the cemetery. I haven't been here in so long, the guilt weighs heavily on me.

It's weird, knowing exactly where my father is buried. I don't know when I memorized the route to this gravesite, but at some point, driving to it became natural. I hate that feeling. None of this should ever be natural. But then again, if it wasn't, we wouldn't have Harrison, and I can't imagine our lives without him.

I sit down and stare at the tombstone. The lettering—it's faded or worn. I'm not sure how to describe what it looks like, except to say it's old. Old because my father has been gone for over twenty years, and the only memories I have of him are the stories I've been told over the years. When I close my eyes, I can't remember what he looks like or what it felt like when he would hold me. I can't see his smile or hear his laugh. I don't know why I'm here, other than I know I need to be.

I run my fingers over his name. The tombstone is rough. No longer the smooth feel it had when I was younger. I wonder if this is something Peyton and I need to take care of, if the stone needs to be polished or something.

"Hey, Dad," I say to the air. "I'm sorry it's taken me so long to visit. Life's been crazy since the last time I was here, but I guess you already know that. My Ben's sick, Dad, and I'm scared. I know I have to trust science, but sometimes science fails, and I'm just so scared it's going to fail. Thinking this way is so unlike me. I always tell people to put a positive spin on things, but I'm having trouble following my own advice."

A family arrives and makes their way toward their loved one's resting place. I watch them for a minute before turning my attention back to my dad. "Dad, you have to promise me, if you meet Ben, take care of him. I love him more than anything and as much as I'd love for you to know each other, I'm not ready. But in case it's his time, please look after him and love him because he deserves it." I spend a few more minutes sitting by my father's grave, contemplating the two paths I have in front of me. One with Ben, and one without. I know in my heart my father, wherever he may be, will take Ben under his wing if it turns out the path I fear most is the one that wins out, but I also hope and pray it won't happen for a long time yet.

When I get back to my grandpa's everyone is there. I hug my mom before making my way to my grandpa. We hold each for a long time. He's old and losing weight. I can feel his bones and he doesn't walk, he shuffles his feet. I'm not ready for any of this. I'm not ready to lose my grandpa, my grandma Bess, or my Ben. Whoever is doing this shit to me needs to stop.

## 18

### BEN

*T*he next morning, I wake to the smell of French toast and a lot of laughter. Elle's side of the bed is cold, and I try to think back to what time she came to bed. When I finally succumbed to my tiredness, she was on the couch with her sister. They were wrapped in each other's arms and watching some movie they claimed made their eyes sweat. Elle offered to come with me, but I told her I'd be okay. Honestly, I'm feeling okay, which only reminds me I'll feel like shit again soon when chemo restarts in a few days. I understand the aggressive approach, but it fucking sucks, and I hate that it's just started. I'm not even close to finishing my first round. Two weeks down and more to go. More infections. More blood transfusions. More hospital stays. More of everything I don't want.

When I get downstairs, I head into the kitchen to find everyone sitting around the table. Well, mostly everyone. Noah stands behind Peyton, Quinn stands behind Katelyn, and Liam stands behind Josie. Elle's holding Oliver, although he's sitting on the table, and Michael's trying to entice him to crawl over to him. *This* is my family. As much as I love my mom and brother, the people surrounding this table are the ones who care for me, day in and day out. They always include me in everything. Not as an afterthought, but as a member of their lives.

"Hey, good morning." Elle sits up a little straighter and smiles when she sees me in the doorway. I make my way toward the table and Katelyn stands.

"Sit here. I'll get you some breakfast. Are you hungry?" Katelyn asks.

"I am, actually." It's been a while since I had hunger pangs. Mostly, Elle forces me to eat something. It must be the strong scent of cinnamon or something. Ever since I started chemo, my senses have misfired. Not necessarily a bad thing since Quinn is currently waving his hand in front of his face and Elle's trying to pawn the baby off on him.

"Nope," Quinn says. "I'm not doing it."

"You need to get ready for when Nola has a baby."

"I'll hire a nanny," he says as he backs away. Peyton stands and takes the baby, but Noah's turning green. He wants no part of the soiled diaper either. I'd volunteer, but no. When Peyton passes me, I reach out and touch Oliver's chubby cheek. He gives me a smile. He's the luckiest baby in the world to end up with the Jameses.

Katelyn sets a plate down in the spot she vacated and tells me to come over. Elle slides into Peyton's empty seat to sit next to me. "How are you this morning?"

"Actually, I feel almost normal, minus the port sticking out of my bicep."

"Your cheeks are pink. This is a good sign. Do you have a fever?"

I shake my head. "Nope." I add maple syrup to my breakfast and look at the jar before I set it down. "This doesn't look store bought."

"It's not," Elle says. "We picked it up while in Vermont. It's from a cute little place called Bennett's Tree Farm."

"It's cute. I like the covered bridge on the bottle."

"How did you sleep, Ben?" Michael asks. "Is the room okay?"

"It's perfect. I must've crashed hard. I don't remember you coming to bed," I say to Elle.

"That's because the twins fell asleep on the couch," Katelyn says. "When I woke, they were snuggled together and sound asleep. I don't know how long I stood there and just watched them but seeing them like that brought back so many memories from when they were little."

"I'm sorry for not coming up," Elle says. She rests her hand on my leg under the table.

"It's okay. I hope you slept well."

She tilts her head back and forth. "Neck hurts and Peyton snores."

"I do not," she says loudly as she comes back into the room with Oliver. He squeals and says "mama" when he sees Katelyn. Her face lights up as if that's the best sound she's ever heard. If anyone is ever meant to be a mother, it's Katelyn.

"We gotta run. I need to go back to Whimsicality." Josie stands. "We'll see you all for dinner." She and Liam say their goodbyes and head out the door, and then Katelyn takes Oliver from Peyton to put him down for his morning nap. Michael says he needs one too. I know I just woke up, but a nap sounds good, especially outside on the back deck where the porch swing is. This is one of the reasons I wanted to be here instead of in Malibu. While I love where I live, there's something about the comfort of a home that's filled with love. Michael's house is like this. It's where I grew up and I love it here.

As soon as Katelyn and Michael are out of the room, Quinn and Noah sit down. I take a few more bites before my stomach starts to protest, but I don't push my plate away. I don't want to alarm Elle and doing so will have her asking if I'm okay. The truth is, I won't be okay for a long time.

"Ben, what are you doing today?" Quinn asks.

"Oh, let me see," I open the calendar app on my phone and stare at the day. It's blank. I'm sure they know this, but where's the fun in giving them the answer right away. "Let's see, boys. It looks like at ten I'm scheduled for a massage and at noon, pedicure. Depending on what you want to do, I may be able to squeeze you in between two and four. Not sure what time Elle wants to have dinner." I set my phone back onto the table and glance at my friends. Their expressions are stoic.

Quinn throws a napkin at me and laughs. "Glad to see you haven't lost your sense of humor."

"Nope, only my balls."

Everyone looks at me and then away. There's an awkward silence as no one knows what to say and I hate it. I want them to laugh. I want them to tease me when I give them an opening.

Finally, Noah starts to grin. "No Balls Ben!"

Quinn snorts, Elle coughs, and Peyton busts out laughing. "Oh, God. I am so sorry. I shouldn't laugh."

"But it's fucking funny, and if I don't laugh, I'm going to go insane," I say to my friends. "I think for me to get through this, I need to be able to joke about it. Deep down, I know it's not funny, but I need the laughter."

Elle takes my hand in hers. "We'll do our best."

"Well, the reason I asked is because Noah and I want to

take you someplace," Quinn says. "So, if you're up for a little guy trip, we'll leave in about ten minutes?"

Part of me feels like I need to ask Elle, but her squeezing my hand is all the reassurance I need. "Yep, give me a few minutes and I'll be ready."

Elle follows me upstairs and starts to strip the bed while I get dressed. I put my clothes in the pile she's created and get dressed. "Do you need me to do the laundry?" I ask her.

"Nope. Go have fun with Noah and Quinn. Just promise me, nothing dangerous or stupid. I love my brother and Noah, but they're dumb boys sometimes and I have no idea what they're planning."

"I promise." I take a step toward her and then stop. In my mind I was going to kiss her, like I would've done any other time, but our dynamic has changed and we're not there, at least not yet. We're friends and I don't know what I'd do without her. However, the problems we had before are still there, festering under the surface. They didn't magically go away because I have cancer and she's sticking by my side. I give her a smile and grab my sweatshirt before she reminds me I need one.

Downstairs Noah and Quinn wait for me in the living room. They give Michael a kiss on the cheek and tell him they'll be back to watch the game later. Outside, we pile into an old truck, with me sitting in the middle.

"Who's truck?"

"It's my dad's," Noah says. "He's had it since he was a teen. He's put some money into it, to keep it running. Lets me borrow it for special occasions."

Quinn cackles. I know I'm missing something, but I don't even care. I'm out with my friends and it feels good to be free. Right now, I'm going to pretend I don't have cancer. After Noah takes a couple of turns, I realize where we're going. Finally, on the last turn, he pulls onto the dirt road, through some tree coverage, and then into the opening. Before us, is the base of the water tower. It's empty and no longer in use. Liam bought the land, so he could preserve the water tower. The town was going to tear it down, but the memories here are too much, for everyone.

We get out of the truck. Noah grabs a backpack, and I can hear bottles clanging together. I can't drink, even though I'd love to get hammered right about now. Quinn climbs the steps first, and then me, followed by Noah. We sit and let our legs dangle. Noah unzips his backpack and hands me a bottle of Coke. I can't help but laugh.

"We know you can't drink, but we wanted to come out here and hang. You know, away from the girls."

"I appreciate it."

I lean back and look out over the treetops. I remember the first time Elle brought me here. I was so nervous. I'd heard about the water tower and how it was a rite of passage for seniors. But not Elle. She made it her place from day one. She used to say she felt close to her father, and since he pretty much found this place with Liam, she was allowed to be here whenever she wanted.

The three of us chug our Cokes and then send the bottles sailing into the back of Liam's truck. The shattering of glass is cathartic. I want to do it again, but guzzling soda isn't the same as beer.

"We haven't told anyone yet, but Peyton's having trouble getting pregnant," Noah says, taking me a bit off guard. He out another Coke, opens it, and takes a sip. He holds the bottle out and looks at what's left. "We've gone through a ton of testing. I've got the swimmers. She has the eggs. But the damage from the car accident might be the issue. No one knows this, so please don't repeat this, but she's had two miscarriages already. I don't know how to help her through them, the second was worse than the first. Both times, the doctor said she wasn't very far along, but that doesn't matter. She was pregnant and lost the baby. Twice." Noah finishes his soda and throws it toward the truck. "I really need a beer."

"I'm sorry, Noah," Quinn says. "I can't even imagine what it's like to go through that. Just know that if and when it happens, I'll be excited to be an uncle. Nola and I have discussed this and neither of us want kids right now though, although I really love all the practice we're getting for when we do. She's got nieces and nephews and every time we head to her parents, they remind us it's okay to wait." Quinn pauses. "Our parents don't think so, but whatever. Nola's sister is keeping her parents busy, and my parents have Evelyn and James, and now Oliver."

"Well, shit," I say. "You're having all the sex." I look at Quinn and his eyebrows waggle. I shake my head. "And you," I don't say anything to Noah because what can you say to someone who is going through what he is. "I had to jack off into a cup so I could freeze my sperm so that one day, if I want to have kids, my wife or whoever can use my sperm to create a baby in a Petrie dish." I look at my bottle and say, "Yep, a beer is definitely needed. Fuck, I can't wait to have one."

"I had to jack off," Noah says. "Before the first miscarriage, we went to a specialist because we've been trying since before the wedding, and Peyton wanted to make sure we're doing our part. They sat me in a room with porn and a cup. It was the most awkward thing ever."

"I got porn on an iPad in the hospital bathroom before surgery. And only thanks to Elle. Even though we're not together, she wanted to make sure my future wife could have a baby."

"Wow, Elle's really changed since all of this," Quinn says.

"I don't give her enough credit," I tell them. "It's easy for me to put everything on her because of what happened before. I was wrong to push a wedding date when I knew how important it was for her dad to walk her down the aisle. I tried to take that away from her and it was wrong." Now it's my turn to finish my soda. I send the bottle flying.

"Fuuuuck, we have company," Quinn says as a SUV pulls in.

"It's my dad," Noah says.

Liam gets out of the car and marches toward the tower. He's a man on a mission. He stands below us and looks up. "What are you doing?"

"Therapy session," Noah says.

"Are you guys drinking?" Liam asks.

"No, just soda." Quinn holds up his bottle, but I doubt Liam can see it.

"I'm not so sure Ben should be up there."

"He's just living his best life," Noah yells down. "And we're not drinking."

Liam looks over his shoulder and then back at us. "Your mothers are on their way here, looking for you. I suggest you get down to the ground before they get here. I don't want to be on the receiving end of either of their wrath."

"Shit, we better go." Noah stands and lends me a hand. He goes down first, and then I follow. My feet are on the ground when another car pulls into the clearing. Both moms get out of the car and Quinn mutters under his breath.

"We'll take care of this, just don't listen as we play the 'our friend has cancer' card."

"Use it and abuse it," I tell him. "Anything to keep us from getting yelled at."

Honestly, the guys shouldn't get into trouble for including me in their afternoon plans. I'm happy they did, and we didn't do anything my doctor wouldn't approve of. The three of us make our way over to Liam, Josie, and Katelyn. Katelyn gives me a once over and then glares at Quinn.

"It was my idea," I blurt out. "Everyone knows the water tower is the place you go when you have a problem. I needed to break some stuff and the guys volunteered to bring me. Everything's good here."

This must satisfy the moms because after some muttering they go back to their car and tell us to get our butts home right away. In the truck, Noah thanks me for taking the blame, but assures me it wasn't necessary. He says he's not afraid of his mom.

"But you're afraid of mine," Quinn says, laughing uncontrollably.

He's right.

# 19

## ELLE

"*S*top pacing," Peyton says. "You're making me nauseous."

"I can't help it. I'm nervous."

"Noah and Quinn aren't going to let anything happen to Ben."

"I know, but I still worry."

Peyton closes the book she's reading and pats the spot next to her on the couch. I sit, with a heavy sigh, and keep my eyes on the front room window. "How are things?"

"Horrible," I tell her. "I want to fix him and make everything better, but I can't. I hate not having any control over the situation, and I hate all the waiting. We have to wait for treatment. Wait for the treatment to work. Wait, wait, wait. And then when the waiting is over, we have to see if the treatment worked, which is just more waiting."

"Does Ben see you like this?"

"I try to hide it from him. He doesn't need to worry about me worrying. I don't know if I'm succeeding though," I tell her. "He sees someone who's determined to fight for him when we're at the hospital, and when we're alone, he sees how vulnerable I am. He's my life, and I'm never going to forgive myself if something happens to him."

"The surgeon said surgery was successful, right?"

I nod. "But that doesn't mean it hasn't spread or the chemo isn't working. Next week, he starts his second batch or whatever, and then radiation if needed."

"Don't they usually say round two?"

"No, I think that's reserved for the next time he starts. We're still on round one. It's all so confusing, and the verbiage is so muddled. I hate all the doctor speak and want to scream at them half the time, like talk to us as humans in words we understand. They make me feel stupid."

"You're not stupid, Elle."

"I feel like it sometimes, P. And I feel incredibly helpless. I know I hover over Ben and I'm sure he hates it, but I don't know what else to do for him. Besides, worry."

Peyton takes my hand in hers. "I think what you're doing for Ben is working. This morning, before the guys asked him to go out with them, he looked happy."

"I think being here—as well as you guys being here—is what he needs. The hospital worries me though, what if they're not equipped—"

"Elle, they're equipped. Do you really think Uncle Liam and Aunt Josie have just been sitting on their butts since you said you and Ben were coming? Noah told me, they toured the cancer wing and the chemo room. You know if they felt like it wasn't up to par, they'd tell you to stay in Los Angeles. They're not going to let Ben down. Or you."

Tears fall. I wipe them away with the back of my hand. I lay my head on Peyton's lap. She combs through my hair, much like our mom does when we need her. "How long are you here for?"

"Off and on. Noah will be here a little more than me, but I have some meetings that I can't do over video conference, and I need to meet with the new recruits. I'll be here as much as I can or in L.A. Wherever you are, that's where I'll be."

"I love you, P. I honestly don't know what I would do without you."

"You'll never have to know."

Except, I almost did. When Peyton was in the car accident, I thought I lost her. I felt her absence deep within me. I couldn't explain the immense pain I was in to anyone because they wouldn't understand what it's like to lose a part of you. Peyton's not just my sister, she's half of me and I of her.

Doors slam and laughter rings out. I sit upright and wipe away the rest of my tears. Before I can rush off to the bathroom to splash water on my face, the guys come in. Ben's holding a bag from the local drug store and has a shit-eating grin on his face.

"What's going on?" Peyton asks before I can get the words out.

"Hey, babe." Noah comes over to her and kisses her. "Ben's going bald, so we're going to shave his head."

"And mine," Quinn says from the kitchen.

"And mine," Liam says as he walks through the door.

"Mine too," Mack says when he enters the house after Liam.

"Hey, Mack," I say, and he waves. Seeing him reminds me that I need to ask Peyton what's going on.

"Shaving your head, huh?" I glance at Ben. He shrugs and tries to hide the smile on his face. I had a feeling the guys would do this and turn it into something fun.

"What about you?" Peyton asks Noah.

162

"Of course," he says, but does so as if he's asking his wife for permission. I know Peyton will never tell him no. Not when it comes to family.

"Do you want me to do it?" she asks.

Noah shakes his head. "No, we're going to take turns."

"Okay, just remember Oliver is using the deck to play so make sure you guys clean up all the hair," Peyton says. Noah tells her they will and leans down to kiss her. I should avert my eyes, but the love they have for each other is what you read about in romance books. It's so pure and unadulterated. I'm jealous that Ben and I have to work to have what Noah and Peyton have. They've always been in sync with each other, long before they ever got together.

"Is he out there now?"

"Oh, no," Peyton says. "He's sleeping."

"We'll clean up. I promise," Noah kisses her again and heads to the kitchen to go outside with the rest of the guys.

Peyton and I decide we need to see the shenanigans and join them outside. Quinn already has a chair set up and grandpa has brought out the broom and dustpan. "Grandpa," I say, getting his attention. "Are you going to let the boys shave your head?"

He laughs and runs his hands over what's left of his hair. "Not much left," he says. "And if I shave it off, it won't grow back."

Ben stands next to me, and I put my arm around his waist. "Did you have fun earlier?"

He nods. "We did. Lots of guy talk."

"Oh, boy."

He laughs. "It's all good."

"Who's first?" Quinn asks before turning the shaver on. I don't know why, but Quinn and this mechanical clipper thing gives me anxiety. I join Peyton at the front of the chair, with our phones poised ready to capture all of this. Someday, we'll share this moment, but not anytime soon. Maybe when Ben has a clean bill of health, then it'll be time to celebrate, and we can look back on this and laugh.

I'm surprised when Liam sits down and tells Quinn to cut it all off. Strip by strip, Liam's hair falls to the deck. When he's done, Mack sits down next. After Noah cuts his hair, Mack takes a bunch of selfies, making us all laugh. He's a cute kid, and I can see why Betty Paige is smitten with him. Quinn's next and Mack does the honors.

Ben announces it's his turn. He sits down, removes his hat, and my heart sinks a bit. He's already lost some hair. I've seen the clumps in the bathroom garbage but haven't said anything.

Quinn takes over the shaver from Mack, and I start to record. Each swipe brings a wave of tears from me. Ben's not the sporty type, like Noah or Liam, who have had their heads shaved time and time again. He loves his hair and has always prided himself on having the latest style. I've always loved the slight curl the ends have and will miss playing with them. Some say, after chemo and hair starts to grow back, it'll come back differently. Either in color or texture. I can't imagine Ben as a blond or with straight hair. I'm so used to the dark locks.

Ben stands and runs his hand over his somewhat smooth head. Everyone claps for him, except me. I hug him tightly. His tears wet my shoulder. I tell him everything will be okay. I don't know if it will be, but I have to keep telling myself things are going to turn out for the best. If I dwell on the negative, those thoughts are going to eat away at me, and Ben doesn't need that from me.

Ben kisses the top of my head. I use this as my cue to step away. I hide my tears from him. He knows I'm crying, but I still turn away. When I look back at him, I smile. "Bald looks good on you."

He laughs. "Remind me to buy some more hats. I think I need a new collection."

"Absolutely. Maybe Peyton will send you some new Pioneers gear."

"Yes, I'll do that as soon as Noah's done shaving his head."

Ben stands next to me while Liam shaves Noah's head. Peyton's broadcasting live from Noah's Instagram account. She doesn't tell his fans why he's doing it, out of respect for Ben, but tells everyone they need to go make a donation to The V Foundation. I join the live and watch the comments pour in, asking if Noah has cancer or if it's his dad. Peyton answers them by saying it's a family friend and their concern turns to Ben, although they have no idea who they're praying for. Someone suggests this should've been a fan event, and while that could've raised money for the foundation, no one had thought that far ahead. When Noah's hair is all on the ground, he gives his fans a close-up, and more comments pour in.

Liam jumps into frame and the comments move so fast I can't keep up with them. Father and son compare their shaved heads, and then Quinn makes an appearance. I look at Ben, to see if he's going to join them, but he shakes his head. One look at him, compared to the three of them, and you'll be able to see who they did this for. Noah finally bids a farewell to everyone, and Peyton ends the livestream.

"Damn, we did not plan this very well. We could've turned this into a massive fundraiser," Liam says.

"Right, we could've had the team to do it or something."

"Would they do it for someone they don't know?" Ben asks.

"In a heartbeat," Noah says. "They're always looking for something to do, and this is right up their alley."

"Well, we missed the boat," I say, hoping to curb anyone from saying "next time". If I have my way, there won't be a next time.

Quinn and Noah stay outside and clean up, while the rest of us make our way back into the house. Peyton says she's calling the moms to talk about dinner.

"Elle, do you mind if I borrow you for a minute?" Liam asks.

"Just sixty seconds?" I joke.

"More like thirty minutes. I want to show you something."

I glance at Ben, who tells me he's fine and follow Liam outside. He holds the door of his SUV open for me. Once he's behind the steering wheel, I ask, "Where are we going?"

"I want to show you the studio."

"Oh." I'm slightly caught off guard. I wasn't expecting him to even give his new studio a second thought where I'm concerned. It's a quick drive downtown and once we park, we run into my mom and Josie, whose arms are full of bags. We help them put the food in the back of my mom's rental.

"You cut your hair," Josie states.

"Uh . . ."

"Oh my, they all did it, didn't they?" Mom asks and I nod.

"Except Peyton, Grandpa, and me."

"Oliver?" Mom asks. I look at her oddly.

"Um, he barely has any hair." I remind her. "Besides, he was sleeping through all of it."

She puts her hand over her chest, relieved.

"Mom, seriously, do you think Peyton and I would've allowed the guys to cut his hair? Geez, way to trust us."

"I do, it's just—"

I shake my head at her, while Liam laughs. "Come on, Elle." We leave my erratic mother and her best friend and head up a staircase. At the top of the stairs, the hallway splits off. There's a photography studio, a dentist office, and another flight of stairs. The sign on the door we're standing in front of says FMG Records.

"FMG Records?"

Liam unlocks the door and turns on the light. The space is small, quaint, and set up similarly to the studio we use in Los Angeles.

"This one time, when I was eighteen or so, I knew Josie was going to be my forever girl. When I decided to open the studio, I needed a name. I tried using our initials, but nothing worked, and then one night, it hit me. I changed the letters around and created FMG Records."

I look at the equipment and run my finger over the sound board. I miss my groups and miss being with them. "Why did you bring me here?"

Liam sits on the stool and motions for me to sit in the producer's chair. "I want you to work for me while you're here."

"I'm not working right now."

"I get it, but hear me out. Ever since I moved back, more and more, I find talent playing at Ralph's, and the bars in Allenville. Some of them are really good, but I don't have the time or believe it or not, the knowledge to get them to the next level. You have to remember, I was discovered. Someone helped me create a demo, introduced me to the right people, set up gigs at bigger venues. This is what I see FMG Records doing for people."

"I think this is great, Uncle Liam, but I already told my bands that I'm not working, remember. You and dad are supposed to be helping me out. I can't ditch them for new talent."

"We are one hundred percent on board with helping, and I'm not asking you to ditch. I'm asking you to help me, while I'm helping you. The talent is here, I just need you to discover it, help them cut a demo, and get the ball rolling. The 4225 West team will do the rest."

"I don't know," I tell him. I'm excited and love the opportunity, but I promised Ben.

"What if we bring your bands here?" he asks. "Plum is almost done and this is a great place for them to record their full album. Quinn can get his band here and Talking Til Dawn is still working on getting a hit. They could play the local bars, maybe set up a benefit for cancer, and we can have them play with Sinful Distraction."

Now, I'm interested, but I won't do anything without Ben's approval. He's calling all the shots now. "I need to talk to Ben," I tell my uncle. "It has to be something he's okay with because I promised I'd be there for him."

"Honestly, I could use him as well. I need someone to run our social media, and it's a great work from home type job. Right now, Betty Paige and Mack are doing that new video app for me, but the rest just sits there."

"Let me talk to Ben. You know I want to say yes, but not without him. I've learned my lesson about putting my career first over him. I can't lose him."

Liam tells me he understands and says we should get back home before our phones start ringing. He shows me the rest of the new spaces and takes me to the top floor where there's a vacant apartment and a small dance studio.

"Too bad Aunt Yvie isn't here."

"Oh, believe me," he says. "I've tried to entice her back. There's a gym going in down the street and I keep sending pictures to Xander."

"Why are you trying to get everyone to leave Los Angeles?" I ask as we walk back down the stairs.

Liam shrugs. "It's weird. I have great memories there, obviously, but since being back here, Beaumont is home, and I want my home to thrive. I want people to come here, to spend their money here."

"Uncle Jimmy will never move here," I say as Liam holds the door to his SUV open for me.

"He might, but Eden won't."

We make idle chit chat about Plum on our way back to my grandpa's. Liam tells me he loves their sound and can't wait to work with them as well as telling me how much fun my dad is having on tour. I can't say I'm not jealous, because I am, but Ben's happiness is more important.

When we get back to the house, we find everyone outside, including Betty Paige, who's carrying Oliver around on her hip. Liam and I grab plates, and I find a spot next to Ben.

"Did you eat?"

He nods.

"How much?"

"Elle," he says my name as a warning.

"Ben," I repeat his tone. "You need to eat. How much did you eat?"

He shakes his head. "I don't need a babysitter."

"Nope, you don't. But you do need nutrients. You've already lost noticeable weight. What can I get you?" I ask him. "There's potato salad, baked beans, chicken, some skewer things. I saw pie. Chips and dips. Anything, Ben. I just need you to eat."

169

He relents and gives me a couple items that sound good to him. I get it, his taste buds are all out of whack and nothing sounds good. Unfortunately, the alternative is a feeding tube, and I don't want that for him.

I bring him back a plate with a little of everything he asked for. I'll be happy if he eats what I give him at this point. I peel some chicken off the bone and hand him a piece. Thankfully, he takes it.

"Where'd you go?" he asks.

"Remember when we came through town yesterday and Liam told us what he had done with the building?" Ben nods. "He took me to his studio."

"Oh?"

"He wants me to find talent in Beaumont and help them make demos." I fill him in on everything Liam said, and how Ben could work as well.

"Are you going to do it?"

I shake my head. "I'm not working, remember."

"I think you should."

"I don't want to leave you, Ben. This is where I need to be."

He leans over and kisses my forehead. "And I'm here, surrounded by family. I think if we're here, you should do what makes you happy."

I open my mouth to say something, but he holds his hand up.

"I can do my part and we can create together, like we used to. Being here, things are different. I'll never be alone."

"That's very true." I look around at the big family we have.

"Besides, it'll give you something to do while I'm sleeping." He laughs.

"I'll think about it."

"Sure, you will," he says. "That's code for you'll push it aside because you think it's the right thing to do. I'm telling you, take the job. I want you to do what you love while we're here. Besides, you'll be five minutes away, and no tours."

"No tours," I tell him.

"Do you think you can show me the studio later?"

"Of course, but you have to do something for me." I eye his plate.

He rolls his eyes. "Yeah, yeah."

## 20

### BEN

*I*t's been three weeks since we returned to Beaumont. The second round of chemo or my next batch, whatever I'm supposed to call it, is over and this is my down week. Although, with it being Friday, I only have the weekend to enjoy myself before I start all over again. The first few days are okay, but by mid-week, I'm exhausted. Mentally and physically. Not to mention I hardly eat because throwing up isn't fun. The only food I can keep down as of late is soup, and I'm sorry but there's only so much soup a guy can take. Unfortunately, the alternative is a feeding tube, which Elle keeps threatening me with. I know I'm not getting enough to eat but forcing myself only makes me feel sicker.

Everyone's in town this weekend, and by everyone, I mean Nola's here, along with her brother, Rhett. He was on a business trip and thought he'd stop in for a few and check out the mysterious Beaumont. It'll be nice to get to know him a little. Quinn seems to really like him. Noah and Peyton are also here, although Noah hasn't left since I returned. I have to admit, we've never been particularly close because he's five years older than me, but he's been a good friend these past few weeks and has even taken me to chemo. I told him he could drop me off and pick me up later, but he stayed in the waiting room and bugged the nursing staff for the entire duration of my treatment. He wanted to make sure I had enough to read while I was sitting in the chair. Unlike Los Angeles, I'm the only patient in there most days, and I have to say, I envy the people who only go once a week. I know eventually that'll be me, but until then I'm going to be jealous of them. Their recovery time is much easier than mine.

Elle's gone back to work—sort of—and when I'm feeling up to it, I go with her. Liam's studio is small, and really only meant for one artist to come in and record at a time. Unless they're invited by Elle or Liam, the studio is a pay by the hour place. Artists can come in and record themselves singing and make a CD, but they're on their own. Elle has brought in a couple people she's come across at Ralph's, but one wasn't willing to work with her because she didn't have any "big" acts tied to her name. When Elle told Quinn this, he cackled, and proceeded to tell anyone who would listen he's a nobody in the music industry. I think he's pretty proud of himself with his newfound status. Usually, he's Harrison James's son. It seems mainstream media forgets Quinn's his own person.

Being at the studio is fun though. I like to watch Elle work. Beforehand, when we were in Los Angeles, she'd be in her office or in the production booth, and I'd be in mine. Very rarely could I sit and pay attention to how she works. She's extremely determined and focused, and I find her to be kind to the artists she brings in. She has an eclectic taste in music, which I find refreshing.

The first time I ever sat at the front desk in Liam's

studio, the phone rang. He has a landline. Once I saw it, I fully expected a rotary phone, but it's this crazy contraption with caller identification, hold buttons, and multiple lights that flash in red, green, and white. I made the mistake of answering the phone one time and having to set up a schedule for someone who wanted to use the recording equipment. An admin assistant, I am not, but I tried. Thankfully, Betty Paige told me to let the calls go to voicemail and she'll take care of them when she's out of school. She comes in every day and on the weekends and mans the phone, books out the studio, and collects payments. She told me it's better to work for her dad, than her mom. I've half expected Mack to be there, learning the guitar, but he spends most of his time at the photography studio across the hall. Taking photos is his passion, according to Liam.

I've also found out that Mack is living with the Westburys full-time now. Nick went to South Africa at Christmas and hasn't returned. I get the sense Liam is put off by this, but he doesn't let it show around Mack. By all accounts, Liam is playing dad to a very impressionable young man, who is a three-sport athlete, part of a student government, learning to drive, and taking photography lessons. Elle says Mack is also a straight A student and won't do anything to mess up his relationship with Liam and Josie.

Speaking of Elle, she's stressed. I can see it in her eyes. It's almost as if some light is gone from them and it breaks my heart. I try to assure her, I'm fine. That I'm playing Star Wars with the tumor and totally beating its ass, but I don't think my words register all the time. At night, when we lie in bed, the worry she feels shows on her face. I wish I could do something to help her, but the words I say fall flat. I can't tell Elle that I'm okay, because she knows I'm not. It's like I'm stuck between a rock and a hard place.

Noah and Quinn come into the house, dressed for the lake, in shorts and T's. They smell like they've bathed in sunblock. The one odor I can still smell perfectly well.

"Are you ready?" Noah asks.

"For what?"

"To go to the lake," Quinn says. "We're all going."

"I'm not," I tell them. If they didn't clear it with Elle, it's not happening. Like it or not, she's my boss and I'll do whatever she says. If it means I'm emasculated by letting her control my life, then so be it. She's trying to keep me alive and somewhat healthy.

"Elle knows. She's going to," Quinn says. "She didn't tell you?"

"No, she didn't." Clearly. I get up off the couch and climb the stairs slowly. They're hard to manage sometimes and usually once I come down them in the morning, I stay downstairs. The many naps I take happen on the couch or in Grandpa's recliner. He had Liam move it so it faces the window, and I can look out and see what the neighbor kids are doing. Honestly, as nice as it is, it makes me feel like I'm eighty years old.

I find Elle sitting in a chair by the bedroom window. Her head is back and she's letting the sun beat down on her face. "Am I interrupting?" I ask after tapping lightly on the door.

She opens her eyes and looks at me. "Not at all," she says. "What does Grandpa say when he's napping—just resting my eyes." Elle turns her face back toward the sun and closes her eyes again. "The sun feels good."

"Speaking of, did you tell Quinn and Noah we'd go to the lake?"

"Mhm," she hums. "Liam rented a boat or a mini yacht for tomorrow. We're all going out there."

"Uh, apparently it's today."

Her eyes shoot open. "What? Liam said Friday."

"Today is Friday," I tell her, and as if she doesn't believe me, she picks her phone up off the nightstand and looks at the date.

"Shit."

"So, we're going?"

Elle nods. "Yep. Crap. I can't believe I lost a day."

"Well, I mean technically it feels like we're on vacation. I haven't had chemo this week, so we're resting."

Elle stands and goes to the closet. She grabs her tote bag and then goes to the dresser we share and takes out her swimsuit, a pair of shorts, and a shirt. "So, the plan is to go to the lake today. Everyone is going, and like I said, Liam has a boat. We're going to hang out, have some fun, eat, play some games, and just relax by the water. Liam's bringing some inner tubes. Oh, and my dad is supposed to be in town today, so Mom and Oliver will join us later."

"Sounds like fun. How come you forgot to tell me?"

Elle stands there with her clothes in her hand. "I don't know," she says with a shake of her head. "It slipped my mind. I guess maybe in the back of my mind, I thought the guys would tell you as they'd be here at some point after they brought it up. No ill intent meant, if that's what you're getting at."

"I'm not. Just curious if you want to go, is all."

"I do. Do you want to go?"

I nod. "I'll get changed and pack all my crap."

Elle laughs, but it's not funny. I swear I take a med kit wherever I go, just in case. There are so many "just in case" scenarios right now that it's better to have some sort of kit on hand. Elle keeps everything centrally located in the bathroom, so it's really a matter of zipping the bag and taking it with me. When I get back to the bedroom, my swim trunks are lying on the bed, along with a T-shirt, a long-sleeved shirt, and a pair of sweatpants. She knows I'm going to get cold.

"Thanks for getting this stuff out."

"Of course. I'll meet you downstairs." She lingers in the room for a moment and then gives me a soft smile. She's hard to read sometimes, but part of me thinks she wants to kiss me, more than the pecks we share occasionally. I know I miss being her person, but she hasn't told me how she feels about us since I told her about the cancer. I sort of miss the fighting because it meant we were talking about our feelings. Now, it seems we only talk about how I'm feeling, which is pretty shitty most of the time.

Elle drives us over to the lake in her rental. We could've ridden with any of the others, but I don't want to burden anyone if I need to leave. When we get there, our large group of family and friends have taken up a sizable space near the lake.

Katelyn's in the water with Oliver. He's in one of those baby floaties with an umbrella to protect his head. Plus, he's wearing a hat. It's funny how many precautions people take with their babies but forget about themselves.

At the end of the dock, Liam climbs off the boat he's rented for the day. I didn't even know he had a captain's license, but it doesn't surprise me. He's a jack of all trades, it seems.

Elle and I claim a couple seats in the shade. After setting our stuff down, we go help set up the food table. I catch Elle smiling when I steal a piece of fruit. It's weird to think that me eating brings her joy.

HEIDI MCLAUGHLIN

After we eat, Liam offers to take people tubing. Noah passes, but Mack, Paige, Quinn, Nola, and Rhett head out. Most of us gather on the dock to watch them and cheer when Liam is able to dump one of them into the water. Next year, I'll be out there, I tell myself. I won't be this weak man who needs to rest every so often. A year from now, things will be different.

Elle sits on the dock and sets her feet in the water. I do the same. Something pokes my leg and when I pull it out of the water, I don't see anything.

"What's wrong?"

"I think I got bit by a fish," I tell Elle through laughter.

She laughs hard, harder than I've seen her laugh in a long time. "You gotta watch out for those trout."

"Right?" I put my arm around her and pull her toward me. Before she can rest her head on my shoulder, my finger and thumb hold her chin so I can look into her eyes. "Thank you."

"For what?"

"For caring. For being here for me."

"I love you, Ben. There's no other place I'd be."

I close the distance and press my lips to hers. Her small intake of breath spurs me on. My tongue touches the edge of her lips, and her mouth opens for me. Kissing her like this brings back a flood of memories and emotions. I'm so in love with her, it hurts.

"I love you, Elle," I say after we part. Her eyes light up. It's like those words have brought back the spark that seemed to have dimmed over the past couple of months. I did that. I took away the glow, and now I need to work to return it. I miss seeing the glimmer of light she used to carry with her.

## 21

## ELLE

*B*eing at the lake yesterday was refreshing. It was like old times, and when Ben kissed me, the butterflies I have felt all my life when it comes to him, resurfaced with such vigor. I find myself wondering why I ever waited so long to act on them. Deep down, I know it's because he was my best friend, and accepted every flaw I have without asking me to change who I am. Crossing the line from friendship into something more was the scariest thing I had ever done. I feared we wouldn't work, and I was right. The first major fight, and Ben wanted to quit. I know he's been invested in us longer, but what happened between us wasn't fair. He was so quick to quit on us and quit on me. This is something we need to work on. I want to be with him forever. I want to have his children. I want to sit by his side, in our rockers, and watch our grandchildren play. If he can't see that in me, then I need to work harder to show him.

Ben sleeps soundly next to me. Since we returned to Beaumont, things have been really great between us. I thought with everyone here, we'd have a disconnect, but we seem to gravitate toward each other. Still, I worry about him, and the germs people bring in and out of grandpa's house. I know everyone wants to hang out, but sometimes, it's a little too much, even for me. I look forward to when it's just the three of us: Ben, Grandpa, and I, and we're watching television or working on a crossword together. It's those quiet moments that bring me calm and afford me a chance to think. It gives me a chance to process everything going on around me whether it's Ben and his cancer, or this job I'm doing for Uncle Liam, which I really think is a front. He doesn't want me to forget my path or stay out of music for too long. He wants me to continue to make a name for myself because more often than not, when you take an extended break, people forget you. When you email an exec that you haven't spoken to in a while, that email tends to get pushed to the bottom of the pile. I can't have that happen, but I also can't leave Ben's side. While my job is crucial and important, Ben's health far outweighs my career right now.

While he sleeps, I take in his features. He's lost weight. It's most noticeable in his face. His eyes are sunken in and his cheekbones more profound. I know some people like this look, but it's not a good look on him. I miss the fullness he used to have and know it will come back eventually, but that eventually is years away. His fight isn't over when chemo stops. He'll have scans and blood tests every few months. He'll worry, as will I, that something's wrong all the time. He might get the slightest fever, or a head cold, and he'll automatically think the worst. At some point, he's going to ask me to stop asking if he's okay, and I don't know if I'll be able to do that.

He has four treatments left and then we wait. We wait for three months, six months, five years. Our lives will be a waiting game until that five-year mark where the doctors will declare him cancer free. Over eighteen hundred days of waiting, while in remission. I can't wait for the day when I can start counting.

Ben stirs and slowly opens his eyes. He looks tired. Exhausted even. "Good morning."

"Morning," he says groggily.

"Did you sleep okay?"

He nods and winces as he starts to roll onto his back. "What's wrong?"

"Just pinched my port."

His port is a necessary nuisance. It's the easiest way to administer his chemo and any other drugs he may need, but it hurts him and seems to always be in the way, even though it's on the inside of his arm. I know I've grabbed it a couple of times by accident. You tell yourself you don't want to think about the cancer and your loved one being sick so you try to act as normal as you can, but the consequence of doing so is inadvertently touching a vital part of their treatment. Knowing it's there makes my stomach queasy, but it's so much worse when I know I've caused him some discomfort.

"I'm meeting Uncle Liam at the studio. We're going to start planning a fundraiser for cancer patients who don't have insurance. I know what this is costing and can't imagine someone not having insurance or the means to pay for treatment. Liam talked about setting up a fund and making this an annual or even semi-annual event. He doesn't want it to be a one-time thing."

"I think that would be really good and could turn into a full-time job for someone. Events like this aren't easy to plan, and then there's the managing the funds aspect. How do you determine who is going to get help and who isn't?"

"I'm leaving all that up to Liam. He has someone lined up to manage distribution. I'm in charge of entertainment."

"Are your bands coming?"

I nod. "Yeah, they're pretty excited. Especially Sinful Distraction. Plus, I'm going to book a lot of local talent. I expect people to travel for this as well. People want to help. Big stars want to help. It would be great to get some major headliners and turn this into a festival of sorts in the years to come."

"Taylor Swift?" Ben waggles his eyebrows.

"You just want to meet her because you have a big crush on her."

"Guilty."

"I don't get it though. She's a blondie and I'm not."

"It's simple. I'm in love with you," he says in the most enduring and sincerest way. "Can I kiss you again?"

I nod and close the distance between us. Ben turns onto this side and cups my face. His lips are chapped and dry from the chemo, no longer the soft lips of before. I don't tell him though. He doesn't need to worry about these small changes while he's fighting the war going on inside his body. I slide a little closer, wanting more. I'm greedy. I can't help it. I've missed Ben so much that these little shared moments between us leave me desperate and hungry for him.

My hand slides under his T-shirt and up his back. When my fingers touch his ribs, he freezes and pulls away. He's lost weight. Too much for my liking. It's why I force him to eat and am trying to encourage him to drink the protein shakes my grandpa does. I know they'll help.

"I'm sorry."

"Don't be. I'm just not comfortable in my own skin at the moment."

"I understand."

Ben keeps his hand on my cheek. "I'll get there."

"I'll wait," I tell him. "You're worth the wait."

"I love you, Elle," he tells me and then kisses me again. His stomach growls and I smile against this mouth. "Well, shit."

I can't help but laugh. "Come on, let's go eat." We climb out of bed, change out of our pajamas, and head downstairs. After I stuff my face and Ben picks at his food, we take turns in the shower. I dress and am about to walk out the door when Ben tells me he is going to come downtown with me because he wants to check out the new bookstore on Main Street.

Downtown is bustling and it brings back so many memories from when we lived here. In the park, across from Whimsicality, there are vendors selling their goods. It's like the Saturday market I visited one time in Portland, Oregon. Through my closed window, I can hear faint sounds of music and wonder who's playing right now.

"Why did we move?" Ben asks.

"My parents, and then college," I remind him as I continue to look for a place to park.

"Why do we stay?"

I parallel park and then ponder his question. It's been on my mind as of late. Part of my job is in Los Angeles. It's where artists flock to, to find record deals.

As well as New York City.

Or Nashville.

Even Austin.

So why not Beaumont?

Liam's words from the other day replay in my mind. Since he returned, more and more artists are coming to Beaumont. Why not turn Liam's record company into something big. It's something I could manage, but it would be hard work. The music industry is a tad more difficult without a major label behind the musician. However, with the popularity of apps and music streaming this could definitely be a thing. Before I get in over my head though, it's something I need to talk to Liam about.

"I can do my job from anywhere," Ben says.

"I know. I'd have to travel though." I glance at him. "I can't expect the bands I manage now to pick up and move or come here to do their stuff. Plus, the studio isn't big enough to fit the likes of Sinful Distraction in there. Can you imagine Hendrix and his larger than life personality?"

"Keane would probably like to raise Chandler here."

"Speaking of . . ." I look at Ben again. "I think he and Dana have a thing going on. I'm not sure and I haven't asked, but Jamie mentioned something about seeing Dana at their grocery store, which is well out of the way from where she lives. And I know Keane has been seeing someone."

"Stay out of it," Ben warns.

"I am, but it'll complicate things. Hendrix is," I sigh, "in love with Dana, but I'm not so sure Dana feels the same way about him. His problem is he can't keep it in his pants. My dad says he reminds him of Jimmy before he met Jenna. Hendrix just hasn't figured out how to fix his issues."

"Maybe he's waiting for the right person to come along."

"Maybe." I turn off the car. We unbuckle, get out of the car, and I meet Ben on the sidewalk. He leans down and gives me a kiss. It's unexpected and very welcomed. He holds my hand, and we walk toward Whimsicality.

There's a line of people waiting to get it. I pause before we get to the door. "You know if we go in there, it's going to be like old times. Josie is going to make us work."

Ben shrugs. "It'll be fun. Besides, it looks like she needs some help."

I beam at Ben. With everything going on, he still wants

to help and not let cancer slow him down. I shrug and he leads me past the people waiting and right to the counter where we encounter a very frazzled Josie.

Her eyes light up when she spots us. "Please tell me—"

"Of course, we are. Where do you want us?" Ben asks.

"Do you guys want to serve? I can take the orders."

"Sure," I say. We step behind the counter and grab aprons.

"Once we get these orders out, I'm going to clean," Ben says.

Ben and I work quickly, getting orders out. We run into a few classmates, who are excited to see us and elated that we're engaged. Neither of us tell them that I refuse to take my ring off even though we've been broken up for months, and we don't tell people that we're living in town for a bit. Once we do, they'll want to hang out and Ben's just not up for that. Right now, it's family. They understand when he needs a break.

The line doesn't die down, but there's enough of a break that Ben is able to bus the tables and get them ready for the next patrons. I tried to get Ben to take a break, but he refused. Now, when I watch him, he's moving slower and probably thinks I don't see him when he rests his knee on the chair for support. The earlier moxie he had is gone.

I know I'm supposed to be upstairs with Liam, but this is fun, and I don't want to leave Ben right now. Working with Ben again is like old times and it's a nice reminder of the life we used to have. Maybe Los Angeles isn't the place for us. Beaumont might not be it either, but we're young enough to figure things out.

When things finally calm down, Josie tells us she can handle the rest. She gives us hugs, promises to come over later with our pay, even though we told her we don't want anything, and sends us on our way.

Back outside, Ben kisses me again and I realize how easy it is to fall into this routine. I'm already there, but know he needs time to figure things out.

"How are you feeling?" The temptation to check his forehead for a fever is there, but I keep my hands to myself. I don't want to embarrass him in front of onlookers.

"I'm great. I'm going to the bookstore," he tells me. "And I'm going to walk around a bit. I'll meet you in the studio later?"

"Sounds good. Be careful, please."

Ben winks and walks away without promising to stay safe. I watch him until he disappears around the corner and smile to myself. I think we're going to be okay.

## 22

## BEN

*a*s soon as I round the corner, out of Elle's sight, I rest against the brick wall. I'm tired. I don't know if it's from busting my ass at Whimsicality or what, but I don't want Elle to hover right now. I bend slightly at my waist and try to catch my breath. I'm sure I have a fever, but I might be overly exerted as well. I know I worked a lot and didn't take a break, but I don't want to admit that cancer is kicking my ass. Well, the chemo is. That shit is nasty and drains every ounce of energy I have. I hate the old adage, what doesn't kill you, makes you stronger. Friedrich Nietzche can kiss my ass with his logic. The cancer, the chemo—it's slowly killing me, and something tells me once it succeeds, there's no coming back from it.

I stay where I am and slip my sunglasses on. I don't want to make eye contact with anyone, especially if they might know me. I ran into enough people while working this morning to last me a lifetime. I could see it in their eyes when they looked at me—they knew I was sick—but didn't ask. I mean, what do you say in a situation like that? "Hey, Ben, what the fuck is wrong with you?" No one is that cold, but a conversation like that makes things awkward. It's just best if no one knows why Elle and I are here.

As I look around, it's amazing to see the changes Beaumont has gone through since I was last here for Peyton and Noah's wedding. The town is thriving, and I feel, in large part, it's because of Liam and Josie's dedication to making sure this is a place people want to live. It could've been so easy for them to pack up and move west to be with the rest of us, but they held fast to the notion that Beaumont is a great place to raise a family. Not going to lie, it felt great working at Whimsicality again. It was just like old times and it's funny how it all came back to me so easily and I never forgot what to do. Of course, running into former classmates wasn't high on my list, but I knew once I put the apron on, it was going to happen. I suppose it's not a surprise to find me or Elle working there, or even Noah and Peyton. When family needs help, you help. It's what everyone is doing for me, and technically, I'm not even family. I'm just a guy who fell in love with a girl, who happens to have the most amazing family I've ever met, and they took me in as their own.

The bookstore on Main Street is new, yet when I finally have the energy to climb the granite stairs, I step inside and take in the décor. The store looks like it's been here forever. The wooden floor could almost certainly be the original one from when the building was built, who knows when, even though I have no idea what was here beforehand. If I remember correctly, the building sat vacant for a long time. Beaumont used to be the town everyone forgot about when it came to upgrading its infrastructure. Sure, people move here, but the town council rarely puts any work into dilapidated buildings. But then again, if my civics classes taught me anything, it's not the local government's issue, but the peoples'. The people of Beaumont have spoken, and they're determined to revitalize their town. Honestly, I'm here for it. I love this town and the more I think about it, the more I want to move back. I think Elle and I can really make a go of it here. I know she'll have to travel, but maybe it's something we do together.

I peruse the bookshelves. There are some classic titles, which entice me. I've always wanted to collect first editions but have never taken the plunge. They're an investment. When I'm with Elle, my cash flow is flexible. Without her . . . well that just doesn't seem possible and I can't even begin to understand what I was thinking in December. I love her. She's my life. I hate myself for kicking our relationship to the curb so fast. Thinking back to that night, I was being so irrational, and I think it's because of my new co-worker and how he described his girlfriend and if he had asked me, I knew exactly what I would want to say. Except I realized then I wanted to call her my wife instead of my girlfriend and I let that notion get the better of me. I will never understand why I needed our status to change immediately instead of sticking with the plan. Maybe, deep down, I knew something was wrong with me and I wanted to be married to her before shit got bad for me. Elle's never pressured me for anything except to accept her for who she is. She never demanded a ring or anything, and all she ever asked was for me to love her, which I can easily do. I'm the one who insisted on more when we were content.

Maybe that's it—we were content.

Was I afraid I'd lose her?

My hand pauses on the spine of an old, tattered copy of *Les Misérables*—a coming of age story about redemption and hidden identities, mixed with a powerful love story among a raging war. Sounds like mine and Elle's life right now with the exception of hiding who we are, although, in a sense, we're doing just that—hiding. I was foolish in thinking I could hide my feelings for Elle. In doing so, I made myself angry and hateful, for no reason other than I wanted to shut off the way I feel about her because I thought it would be easier than admitting I made a mistake. No man wants to ever admit they were wrong, but I was. Still am. Every day I think about telling Elle to forget what I said, but there's damage that needs to be fixed, and I'm the one who needs to fix it. I don't expect Elle to just forget the things I said to her.

There are a couple of tables in this store, as well as a coffee and tea station. I brew myself a cup of coffee and take one of the tables in the front window. It's been a few weeks since I've checked in with my co-workers. Unfortunately, they all know I have cancer. I say it's unfortunate because it's a pity party. We're not close and barely know each other. Prior to my diagnosis I was only in the office a couple of times because we're allowed to work remotely. The camaraderie some people have with their co-workers isn't there for me. Nonetheless, they're all sorry I'm battling for my life right now. While I appreciate the support, the sympathy sucks. I stopped showing my face during meetings so they can't see how much I've changed. No one needs to comment on my looks right now. I know I look sick. I have bags under my eyes that rival parents with a colicky newborn.

After a sip of coffee, I boot up my laptop and send a message to my team. Replies pop up instantly and after a round of "how are you doing" conclude, we talk business. The agency landed a new client and now it's our responsibility to take them from a regional success to a globally household name. Super easy, said no one in advertising. This makes working with bands much easier.

In between answering messages from my co-workers, I decide to start working on a logo for Plum. It's not my job, but I know it'll make Elle happy, and I want to make her happy. Truthfully, working for her was easy. Another mistake on my part by leaving, but there wasn't any way I'd be able to work with her and not be with her. There's no way in hell I'd ever be able to watch her move on and that's a fear I live with every day.

When I'm satisfied with some options for Plum's logo, I sign-off, close my laptop, pack my things up, dump the cold coffee, and make my way to the check-out counter with a couple of new paperbacks. With my new books in hand, I decide to check out the new pet store. I have mixed feelings about stores like this. Are the pets taken care of? Are their cages cleaned? Are the animals fed regularly?

Inside, there's a pen in the middle of the store with a couple of puppies playing with each other. There's one though, who sits in the corner. He looks at his friends and I imagine he's thinking to himself, "What are they doing?" He makes me smile. I reach down and pet him. He leans his head back and looks into my eyes.

My soul.

"Hi, buddy." It's in this moment that I know I want to take this little guy home. But where is home? And how can I train him if I'm puking my guts out every day?

"Would you like to hold him?" One of the employees asks. "We have puppy rooms if you'd like one. You can get to know him."

"Sure, that would be awesome."

The clerk goes inside the pen and the others start to attack her ankles. She doesn't seem to care as she scoops up the little guy and tells me to follow her. "He's a labradoodle," she tells me when we get into the room. "He's had all of his shots and is just waiting for his forever home."

"How old?"

"Three months." She opens the half door to the room, and I follow, only to see there is no place to sit, other than the floor. She sets the puppy down and he sniffs around. She stays there, almost as if she's waiting to see what I'm going to do. I smile and lean against the wall and sort of slide down until I'm seated. "Have fun," she says as she closes the half door.

I reach out and pet his head and he instantly climbs onto my lap and continues to climb until he reaches my face and gives me some kisses and then curls up on my lap. It's amazing how something so innocent can project their love so easily. I'm sold and I never thought I'd want a dog. I pick him up and snuggle his soft fur and pull my phone out to take a picture of us. I send it to Elle with the caption, "he needs a family."

"We gotta get Elle's permission," I tell him. "But something tells me she'll say yes. Maybe she'll come and meet you. I know once she sees your big brown eyes, she'll put you in her bag and take you home."

He looks at me like he understands everything I'm telling him. For all I know, he does. We play for a bit until Elle's text comes in. "Buy him now!"

"Well, would you look at that?" I show him the phone. "She wants you, with no questions asked. Maybe this is a good sign," I tell him. "Maybe you'll be the reason we get back together."

"How's it going?" the clerk leans on the top of the half door and grins.

"Amazing. I'm in love already. How do I go about

buying this little guy?"

Her grin turns into a beaming smile. "Yay, I'm so happy. I'll start the paperwork. What's your name?"

"Is this for ownership?"

"Yes, we document who buys each dog or cat."

"Okay," I pause and wonder if I should include Elle and then remember she's in charge of my future offspring so she should have rights to this guy as well.

"His owners will be Ben Miller and Elle James."

There's a hint of recognition in her eyes. I smile and ask, "Is there a home visit or anything?"

She shakes her head. "The cost of him pretty much assures us that you can take care of him. Besides, the owner knows Elle's family. I mean, we all do. I can't imagine anyone telling her no." Her eyes go wide. "Oh, I didn't mean that the way it sounded."

I smile and shake my head. "No worries. I rarely say no to her myself, so I get it."

"Right. I'll go get the paperwork started."

"Thank you." As soon as she's gone, I pick the little guy up. "Well," I say to the fluff ball. "I guess you're going to need a name." His tongue darts out and licks my nose. "I hope you like the beach because that's where we live, unless we move back here. I think I'll teach you to surf. That would be fun, wouldn't it? Just wait until everyone meets you." He looks at me with longing in his eyes.

"Yeah, they're going to fall in love with you, just like I did."

I start to get woozy and set him down. I can feel him licking my hand or my face, but everything else is fuzzy right now except the ringing in my head.

"Elle," I say her name as if she's sitting next to me before everything goes dark.

## ELLE

*O*nce I lose sight of Ben, I open the door and head up the stairs to FMG Records. Betty Paige sits at the desk and has the phone pressed to her ear and her hand scribbling on a piece of paper. For being a teen, she's one of the best multi-taskers I have ever met. Liam is damn lucky she's so detail oriented because since he opened the studio, it's been packed with artists making demos and hoping to catch his attention, and now mine.

My focus should be on the guy sitting on the stool, strumming his guitar, and singing into the microphone, who's trying to impress me enough that I'll want to work with him, but my attention is on my phone, eagerly awaiting another photo of Ben and this puppy he's found. I have no idea where he is, but from the looks of the image, he's in a room. I do remember seeing a pet store not far from here, but it's new and I know nothing about it. I'm going to assume he's there and has met this most adorable puppy. I never thought we needed a pet, especially a dog, but now I do. The look on Ben's face, the sparkle in his eyes, tells me he needs his little ball of fur, and so do I.

"How was that?" the man on the stool, who's seeking my undivided attention, asks. *Shit.* I look down at my notes to try and refocus myself. His name's Phillip Shaw but plans to go by Jersey as an artist. I like it. It's edgy and creative.

I take my headphones off and contemplate telling him the truth—I wasn't listening—but I know saying this will hurt his ego and I'm not going to do that to this guy. I press the button on my sound board allowing me to talk to him without going into the room. "Let's go one more time and really focus on what the song means to you. You wrote this for a reason, let me hear it. I want to feel the emotions in your voice while you tell the story through the lyrics and your sound."

Phillip or Jersey smiles. "I can do that." I press the record button and once the red light comes on, he starts strumming. As soon as he belts out the first verse I know my feedback, although made up, was right. He's already singing with more emotion. Whoever did this guy dirty is going to know this song's about her once it hits the airwaves, and I'm here for it. I write some notes about adding some background vocalists, drums, and possibly some keys. I can always send this to Jimmy and ask him to fill in with some keyboard work. It's nice to have a well-established band in your back pocket. 4225 West won't ask for payment to play on tracks, which is nice. They have no qualms helping other artists. Royalties and credit—it's all that's needed in return.

When he finishes his riff, I wait a few seconds before I press stop on the recording. I press the intercom button and say, "Come on out here, let's chat."

Phillip comes out and I offer him my seat. The studio is small and there's not a ton of space. It wasn't meant to conduct business in, but I'm making it work. My cell rings and I expect to see Ben's image, but it's an unknown number. I decline the call and turn my attention to Phillip.

"Great sound," I tell him. "I'm going to play around with the recording and see what I can do to sharp . . ." my phone rings again with the same number. I hit decline again. "Sorry, these damn telemarketers are relentless. Anyway, I'm going to sharpen the sound by adding some additional background instruments."

"Maybe you should answer that." He motions toward my phone. The same number is calling again. I sigh heavily. I hate interruptions, more so when people don't leave a voicemail. If I declined you the first time, there's a reason. Leave a message.

I stare at my phone for a long moment and finally pick it up. I answer with a snappy, "Hello?"

"Elle James?"

"Yep, who's this?"

"This is Lynn Willard from Beaumont General. You're listed as Benjamin Miller's emergency contact in his file. I'm calling to let you know he's been brought in by ambulance."

My heart drops and my throat tightens as tears fill my eyes. "What?" I squeak out.

"I don't have much information other than he collapsed at the pet store and they called 9-1-1. The doctors are in with him now."

I still can't process what she's saying. My ears feel like they're full of water and she sounds muffled. My brain doesn't seem to grasp the urgency of what she's telling me.

"I'm sorry, what?" I ask again. Ben just sent me a photo of him and the puppy . . . at the pet store. "Ben's at the pet store buying a dog."

"Yes ma'am," she says. "He collapsed and they called

emergency services. He's been transported to Beaumont General for care."

"Oh, God." I cover my mouth. "I'll be right there." I hang up and apologize to Phillip, telling him I'll be in touch. Grabbing my purse, I head to the reception area where Betty Paige sits at the front desk. "Call your dad and tell him Ben's been rushed to the hospital. And call . . ." I try to think of who else, but no one comes to mind except my sister.

"Don't worry, I'll call my dad and Peyton and let her know, and I'll close up here."

"Thank you, Paige."

For a moment I think about how mature she is for her age, but then all my thoughts are on Ben. Rushing to my car, I go through all possible scenarios. What in the hell happened? Everything has been going so well. How can he collapse? He just sent me the picture of him and the puppy, he looked fine.

*Didn't he?*

I want to look at my phone and analyze the image, but I can't. I need to focus on the road and get to the hospital. My heart races when I have to stop at the red light. I contemplate running it because Ben needs me, but I wait. I'm impatient when the light switches to green and I lay on my horn. I turn my flashers on to let people know I'm in a hurry, but only the car in front of me moves out of the way. I'm sure they're flipping me off, but right now, I don't care. Everything in my gut is screaming that something is wrong. Is this what my mom felt like when she found out about my father?

No, the cops knocked on her door and drove her to the hospital. They came in the middle of the night, while Peyton and I slept in our beds. I don't remember that night or much of my time with my father unless it's through a story or an image. He's an enigma and someone we talk about. When people around town talk about my father, they talk about a man I don't even know. My sister and I know him through pictures and other people's recollection of him. It's weird to think of my father like that, but there's really no other way.

No, this is what it felt like when I got the call about Peyton being in an accident even though I already knew something was off. Her loss is something I would've felt for the rest of my life, and being on a plane, stuck thousands of miles in the air without any communication with my family was the most unbearable and unimageable part of my life that I never wish to experience again. Knowing my sister was fighting for her life gutted me. I felt her pain, her anguish, and I could hear her cries inside my thoughts. When I closed my eyes, I saw it all, without knowing the truth. She is me and I am her. What I feel now is different. Ben's a piece of me in ways only Peyton can understand because she's the same with Noah. I know I have a hard time showing emotion when it comes to Ben because I expect him to know. I expect him to sense what I'm feeling and how much he means to me. It's taken his diagnosis to show me how I need to be better at showing my affection. Everyone needs reassurances in life, Ben is no different. The small touches that I find enduring aren't enough for him. He needs to be told and shown what he means to me. I pray I'm not too late.

I pull into the hospital parking lot and don't slow down when I drive over the speed bumps. The rental car all but bottoms out, but I don't care. The insurance can pay for it if I've done some damage. I park, taking up two spaces and don't bother correcting the car. It can wait. Ben can't. I run into the hospital and almost hit the glass doors because the motion sensor doesn't sense my presence. I have to step back and wave my arms like the frantic woman I am in order for the doors to open. Once inside, I run to the nurse's station.

"Ben Miller," I say through ragged breath. "Lynn something or other called me about Ben Miller. Where is he?"

"Your name?" the man behind the desk asks without making eye contact.

"Elle James."

He stares at me sympathetically and then starts typing. "I'm supposed to ask for your identification, but I went to school with Noah, so I know who you are. Ben's on the fifth floor. ICU."

"ICU?"

"I don't have any other information on my end. They'll explain more upstairs. I've told them you're on your way up." He stands and points down the hall. "Go down the hall, take the elevator to the top. When you come off, take the first left, go down the hall and press the button. One of the nurses will come out and talk to you."

"Thank you."

The elevator is taking its slow ass time getting to the floor I'm on, regardless of how many times I press the button. I know it doesn't help, but it feels good to push my finger against the round disc. When the doors finally open, I wait for the people to get off and step inside. There are four other people in here and I can feel them staring at me. Visions of my mom, standing in this elevator and watching the numbers flash above, play in my mind. Only, my father never made it out of the emergency room. He died there, from his injuries.

I'm the last one in the elevator by the time it reaches the fifth floor. Such a small place compared to the hospitals in

Los Angeles. I guess in some respects this is better. In others, I'm not sure this is the right place for Ben. Everything I agreed to, with his care being moved here, is coming back to haunt me.

I follow the directions from the nurse downstairs and find the button I'm supposed to press. Someone from the other side of the door tells me they'll be out in a minute after they ask my name. After what seems to be an eternity, a doctor dressed in scrubs comes out and calls my name.

"I'm Elle James. Where's Ben?"

"I'm Dr. Franklin," he tells me. "Let's go sit." He motions for me to walk, but I'm frozen in place. I need my mom, my dad, Peyton, or someone to hold me up because my knees are about to buckle.

No, I need Ben.

"I don't want to sit."

He nods and clasps his hands in front of him. "Ben came in with a fever of one hundred four and a severe infection in his leg that spread rapidly. He has sepsis and we're monitoring the damage it's done to his kidneys. Right now, it's touch and go. He's in a medically induced coma at the moment. We're hoping to avoid surgery due to his compromised immune system."

"I don't understand. I've read about sepsis, and we've been careful. How did he get an infection in his leg? The last infection came from his port."

"Ben presented with a very deep gash on his calf. Did he recently cut himself on something?"

I shake my head. "No. We spend most of our time together unless he's getting chemo. He never said anything to me."

"The wound should've been cleaned immediately, and

treatment sought, especially with his compromised immune system."

I nod. "He never said anything," I say quietly. "What's the . . ." I swallow hard. I've done all the readings. I know this is bad. "His uh . . ." I can't bring myself to ask.

"It's too early to say. He's on an aggressive regimen of antibiotics but we're battling his other medical conditions at the same time. It's my hope we've caught it before it's too late."

It's not the cancer trying to kill him this time.

"Can I see him?"

"Yes, come with me."

I follow him into the intensive care unit and to Ben's room. I pause outside his room. I can see him in bed, lying there. In a way, he's being kept alive by the machines. They watch his heart rate, his oxygen levels, his blood pressure, and they pump drugs into his system.

"Jesus," I whisper.

The doctor tells me to sanitize my hands before I go in and I do. He goes over the visiting rules, and I nod, knowing them by heart. I've been here before, but he doesn't need to know this. I sit down and reach for Ben's hand. It's warm, like it was earlier this morning.

"Why didn't you tell me you were hurt?" I ask him as tears stream down my face. I know full well he's never going to answer me regardless of being in a coma or not. He'd do everything he can to save face with me, to appear stronger than he is.

"I don't know what's going on inside of your body, but I need you to fight, Ben. I need you to do what you can to get rid of it because I need you. I need you to be by my side for the rest of my life."

"Ms. James?"

I look up at the nurse standing in the doorway and wipe my tears. She doesn't wait for me to answer or acknowledge her.

"There are people in the waiting room," she says as she looks at the piece of paper in her hand. "I'm to tell you, 'your family is here, princess'."

*My dad is here.*

I get up, kiss Ben on the forehead and tell him I'll be right back. I follow the nurse out of the room and down the hall to the door. She tells me to press the call button when I'm ready to come back in.

As soon as I step outside of the door, my dad has me in his arms. "Daddy," I mutter into the crook of his neck. "He's so sick."

"It's okay, princess. I'm here now." He steps back and looks at me. "You just be strong for Ben; we'll be strong for you."

"When did you get here?"

"About two hours ago. We wrapped up the tour and Plum is back in LA. I came right here."

"Where's Mom?"

"At home with Oliver. She doesn't want to leave him with Grandpa unless Oliver's napping."

I completely understand.

Peyton joins us, and we hug for a moment before Dad puts his arm around me and walks us into the waiting room. The Westburys are there, with the exception of Noah. I thank Paige for taking care of everything at the studio and tell Liam she definitely needs a raise.

Mack steps forward and shows me his phone. It's more pictures of the puppy. "Where did you get these?"

"I was at the store when Ben collapsed," he says. "I had just gotten there and heard the clerk yell for someone to call

9-1-1. I called not knowing it was Ben until I peeked around the corner. I stayed with him until they took him, and I gave the medic your phone number to call."

*The declined calls.*

"Anyway, the clerk said Ben was buying this little guy, so I took some pictures for you, and I told her you or someone would be back to finalize the transaction. So, he's kind of on hold until the end of the day."

I need this dog. I don't know how I'll take care of it if Ben isn't around, but he wants this puppy and so do I. I hand Peyton my credit card and ask her to go back to the store with Mack to get the dog and all the accessories it needs. It's a rash decision, but I don't care right now. That little puppy made Ben's eyes sparkle and I'm going to do what I can to make sure the sparkle returns.

While we're sitting there, I realize I have to call Brenda. It's never fun conversing with her, but she's Ben's mother and needs to know what's going on. As much as I'd love to text her, I'm not that insensitive. I step away from my family and make the call.

"Brenda, hey, it's Elle."

"What's wrong with Ben?"

I inhale deeply, wishing we had a better relationship. "He's in the hospital."

"What did you do?"

*Oh, I don't know, nurtured him, taught him what it's like to have a family.*

"You should come to Beaumont," I tell her.

"So, help me, God. If he dies, I'll sue you."

*Yep, of course you will.*

"It's hard to explain, but he has a bad infection and they've put him in a medically induced coma."

"You know why this is, right?"

*Nope, but you're going to tell me.*

I stay silent.

"If you hadn't convinced him to return to that Podunk town, none of this would've happened. He was just fine when Brad and I were there, and now this."

*Never mind that Ben wanted to be here.*

Before I can respond, my phone is taken from my hand. I stand there and watch Liam, with my mouth open.

"Brenda, Liam Page here. Listen, I don't like the way you're speaking to my niece. My suggestion, get to Beaumont." He hangs up and hands my phone back to me. "I'm sorry, Elle, but enough is enough when it comes to her. Next time, text her. Go be with Ben. He needs you right now."

Liam walks me back to the ICU door and waits with me until the door opens. "Let us know if you need anything, we'll be right here, waiting."

"Thank you," I say as I give him a hug. "I love you."

"Love you too." He kisses the top of my head and urges me through the door.

In Ben's room, the nurse tells me there hasn't been any changes, not that I expected there to be, but I thank her and sit down in the chair next to his bed.

"Mack met the puppy," I tell Ben. "He and Peyton are on their way to get him. I don't know what we're going to do with him right off, but I didn't want to take any chances that someone else could buy him." I laugh. "I don't even know what kind of dog he is or anything, yet when you sent me the picture of the two of you, I knew we needed him. Now we just have to think of a name. It has to be something catchy though and nothing ordinary like Fido or Rover. We should make it unique. Something that will make people comment because of how it stands out."

I rest my arms on the edge of his bed. "Of course, this means you need to wake up so we can do this together. It's not fair to the puppy. I could see it in his eyes, he's already in love with you, just as you are him." I move my head to rest on his hand, thankful there are no tubes or wires coming from it. My tears wet his skin and the blankets covering him. I can't stop them, even if I tried.

Ben needs a miracle.

# 24

# BEN

"*Happy anniversary.*" *I lean down and press my lips to Elle's. She responds in kind and places her hand on the back of neck to pull me closer. I smile against her mouth and try to pull away.* "*Babe.*"

"*It's been forever, Ben.*"

*I can't help but laugh.* "*It's been hours.*" *A lesser man would be upset if his wife didn't remember the last time he made love to her, but I know Elle's joking. It's been an ongoing joke between us since my medicine made me delirious and I'd forgotten her name once. In my defense, I was sick and in the hospital.*

"*Hours to you, feels like months to me, Ben.*" *Elle tries again to pull me on top of her. I oblige, but with no intentions of making love on the couch. Those days are long past us. When you have children running around, they can walk in on you any time. The last thing they need to see is my white ass thrusting in the air.*

*Instead, I lie down next to her and she rolls over onto her side.* "*I can't believe we've been married for ten years now,*" *I say to her while her finger toys with the buttons on my polo shirt.*

*"That's a long time, right?"*

*I nod. "There was a time in my life . . ." My voice trails off. I don't need to finish my sentence because we both know exactly what I'm going to say. There was a time in my life when I thought we wouldn't end up together. Yet here we are celebrating our ten-year anniversary.*

*"Do you remember our wedding?" I ask as I push her hair behind her ear. In all our time together, she hasn't changed, hasn't aged. It's like I'm still staring at twenty-something Elle James.*

*"Do you?"*

*I nod. "I remember you walking down the aisle in your mermaid style dress. You had a veil over your face and held the bouquet Josie made for you. Your dad beamed with so much pride as he walked you down the aisle. It seemed like it took forever for you to get to me though."*

*"Sounds beautiful."*

*"It made me anxious, but truthfully, I didn't care. It prolonged our moment. Some wedding ceremonies are so fast. I'm glad ours was slow."*

*"What else do you remember?" she asks.*

*"I remember how perfect and flawless you looked, just like you look now. Never a hair out of place." I place a kiss on the tip of her nose. "Your hair was curled, and you kept it down, which I love." My finger twirls a strand of her hair. "Our vows, though, sometimes I forget those. I know I told you how much I loved you, and you me. We promised to always be friends, no matter what, and I know you're my best friend."*

*"What did you tell me that day?" she asks.*

"I told you that I'd love you until the day I died, and you said you'd never let me go," I tell her.

"What else?"

"I remember slipping your wedding band on, and thinking how lucky I was you chose me to spend the rest of your life with. You could've had any man out there and you chose me. There have been so many times I've asked myself how or why."

"Did you find the answer?"

I shake my head. "Nope. I'm so ordinary it's unbeliev-able especially when you're you and I'm so plain.

"Who am I?"

"My wife and the mother of my children. Our kids are beautiful because they look like you."

"They must look like you, if they're part of you," she says.

"I hope not. I'm damaged."

Elle stares at me for a long moment. I decide I want to sit outside. "Come on, let's go sit outside on the porch. I want to rock in our chairs and watch the children play."

I take her hand and help her stand. We walk out to the front. The kids are there, playing. We sit in the white rockers and continue to hold hands. "Why's the water so close to the grass?"

"You tell me," Elle says.

"I don't know. Where's the sand?"

"I don't know. Can you find it?"

"Weird. Do the kids seem fuzzy to you?"

Elle shakes her head and looks off into the distance.

"Maybe I have a headache," I tell her.

We continue to rock back and forth. I close my eyes for a bit, hoping that when I open them, everything will be clear. I take a couple deep calming breaths and open my eyes.

Nothing has changed. There's a gray haze covering everything.

I call for the kids to come to me, but they don't. They don't even look up. They continue to play and ignore me. Anger sets in and I look at Elle. "Why are they ignoring me?"

She shrugs. "You have to call them by their names."

I think hard, trying to remember their names, but my mind draws a blank. I look at my wife. Why can I remember our wedding but not our children. "What are their names?"

Elle shrugs again. "You never told me," she says. "It's your dream, Ben. You make our lives the way you want them. I only know what you tell me. I'm only here because you bring me with you."

"You knew your vows," I point out.

"Did I? Or did you tell them to me?"

I think about what she says and become more confused. "I don't think I like it here."

"You can leave if you want."

"Where will I go?"

"Only you know," she says.

Why can't she just give me the answer.

"Whose kids are those?" I ask, pointing to the small group playing. There are three, maybe four . . . no, there are only two of them.

"You tell me they're ours, but I don't know them."

"I want to leave."

"Then you have to wake up."

"How do I do that?"

Elle shakes her head. "I don't know."

"You're not helping."

"I know and I'm sorry. I love you, Ben. Maybe if you believe me, you'll wake up."

"I don't think it works that way."

*Elle smiles.*

*"Why are you smiling?"*

*"Because you want me to."*

*"If I want you to cry, will you?"*

*"Yes."*

*"Weird."*

*"Yes, dreams are weird."*

*"If I wake up, will you be there?" I ask her.*

*"I'll always be there, Ben."*

25

ELLE

We're on day three of Ben being in the hospital. Yesterday, the doctors started weaning him off the drugs that keep him asleep. They said he could wake up at any time, which is great, but it's not good enough for me. I want him to wake up now, not later. I'm so eager to talk to him, to see his eyes, to see his smile, to hear his voice, the waiting is making me incredibly anxious.

Not to mention, I'm stressed. More stressed than I've ever been. Brenda let me know she's on her way and made it very clear that I should pay for her travel expenses. She's probably right. Maybe I should've offered, but she's made zero effort to see her son in all these years, until she needed a place to crash, and she hasn't called Ben once since we came back to Beaumont. I said she could figure it out herself.

The nurse comes in and tells me she needs to give Ben a sponge bath. I want to tell her to take a hike, but the infection on his leg needs to be cleaned. I thought about asking for a male nurse, but I don't want to be a pain in the ass.

She's doing her job. It's not like she's hitting on him or doing anything inappropriate.

Outside, in the waiting room, my dad sits on one of the love seats. I will say, these seats are somewhat comfortable and made from pleather cushions. They're much better than the normal hard plastic the hospital subjects visitors to. I sit down across from my dad with a heavy sigh.

"Where is everyone?" I ask. By everyone I mean my sister and mom. They've taken turns looking after Oliver so one of them can always be here. My dad hasn't left though. The Westburys come and go. Liam stops by in the morning and after he closes the studio, and Josie brings us lunch. I'm super grateful because I hate the food here. You'd think after the hours I've spent in a hospital I'd be used to it by now.

My phone rings and John's name appears. I answer immediately. "Hey, John." Ben and John have such a deep connection. It's like they were meant to meet.

"How's our boy?"

"Still asleep," I tell him. It's better for me to say Ben's sleeping, instead of being in a coma. Coma sounds so formal and scary. "He's getting a sponge bath now."

John laughs. "You know, I've always wanted one, but I'd rather not be hurt enough that I can't bathe myself."

"I hear ya." I let out a sigh. "He's going to wake up," I say. I don't know if I say this for John or for myself.

"Of course, he is."

"Have you given any more thought about coming out here? I know Ben would love it. My dad's band has a private jet. The offer still stands. If you want to come to Beaumont, I'll make all the arrangements."

"Your offer is very kind, Elle. But I have patients here that need my attention."

"I understand," I tell him. "I'll keep you updated on Ben. The doctor's hoping he'll wake up today."

"Thank you. By the way, do you know how he hurt himself?"

I take a deep breath. It took me a solid day to replay everything we'd done in the past week to get where we are today. "We went to the lake last weekend," I tell John. "He put his feet in the water and then complained he got bitten by a fish. My brother went out to the dock we sat on and found rusty nails protruding from the posts. We're assuming Ben scraped his leg against the nail and because his leg was in the water, we never saw the blood."

"Damn. Freak accident."

"I should've known better, but I was just so happy he felt well enough to go out."

"It's not your fault, Elle. Accidents happen. Trust the staff to take the best care of Ben and everything will be okay. As you said, they caught the sepsis early. He can have a nice recovery and live a long, happy and healthy life. Remain positive and call me if you need anything."

"Thank you, John. I really needed to hear those words. I'll call you later."

We hang up and pull my knees up to my chest and hug my legs.

"John seems like a nice guy."

"He is," I tell my dad. "He's been a great advocate for Ben."

"Sometimes those are the people that get us through the challenging times. We don't have to impress them, and they have zero expectations of us. They're there for us, regardless."

"Ben needed John when all of this started. I'm thankful for him. Grateful he was there when Ben needed someone to stand up for him and guide him through the process. He literally held Ben's hand when the diagnosis came in. I should've been there . . ."

"You're here now, princess. These are the moments Ben's going to remember in the long run. He's not going to talk about the time you weren't there. Besides, it was his decision. If I had to go out on a limb, I'd say he regrets it now."

"Regret is such a harsh word, Dad."

He shrugs. "Maybe, but nonetheless, I'm willing to bet he wishes you were there when the doctor told him."

"I feel like I should've insisted we stay in Los Angeles."

My dad comes and sits by me. I lean into him and lose myself in his cologne. He's worn the same one since I've known him. It's comfort. It's home. "I'm scared. I'm scared he's not going to wake up or that when he does, there's so much damage he can't recover."

"I know, sweetie. All we can do is hope and pray the doctors caught the sepsis in time and he'll be okay."

"If you're out here, who's in with my son?"

Brenda's snarky voice rings out over the waiting room. Thankfully, it's empty so no one else has to listen to her.

"Hi, Brenda," I say, trying to sound pleased that she's here. "It's nice to see you again."

She looks at my dad and smiles. My stomach twists. I will never let Brenda be alone in a room with my dad or even Liam or Jimmy. I know she'd try something and when rebuffed, she'd freak out. She's untrustworthy. I know she's Ben's mom and has every right to be here, but having her here makes me sick to my stomach.

"Stop with the niceties," she says. "I know you don't like me."

*Because you just love me.*

"You're Ben's mother. Of course, I like you."

She scoffs.

I look down and see her suitcase. Either she didn't book a hotel, or she came right here. I'm going to think her son means more to her than anything, and she came here from the airport because I'll be damned if she thinks she's sleeping in Ben's room.

"It's good to see you, Brenda," my dad says, and she lights up. I get it. Most people are charmed by him. Still to this day, my mom will say my dad can charm her out of her socks with just one word or wink. Of course, these are things a daughter doesn't want to hear, but I'm happy for my parents.

"Won't you come sit," he suggests. Brenda takes the seat across from us and makes eyes at my dad. I swear I can see her eyes turn into hearts.

"Ben's getting a bath right now," I tell her, breaking her concentration. "When he's done, the nurse will let me know."

"Us," she says as she gives me a pointed look.

"Right." I look away from her, unable to engage her in her antics.

"I want to know what you're doing about his healthcare."

"What do you mean?" I ask her.

"He was in one of the best hospitals in the country and you moved him here, and now he's sick. I looked up what he has on the web. He's going to die from it."

"He won't die," my dad butts in. "The doctor is certain they caught it in time and before the infection did any real damage."

"Certain is not matter-of-fact," Brenda fires back and she's right.

"You're absolutely right, Brenda." As much as I hate saying it, I want to give her credit for looking things up about her son's illness. She deserves that much. "We can only go by what the doctor says, and he feels like Ben has a strong chance of recovering with little to no side effects. Of course, only time will tell, but he'll have care, regardless. As for being here—it's what Ben wanted. After the first infection in his port, he didn't want to stay in Los Angeles or Malibu and asked that we come here. He's happy in Beaumont. It's where he's comfortable. And while Beaumont General may not have the best of everything, Ben does because I make sure of it. The doctor here has been in constant contact with his oncologist and urologist. I can assure you I'm not taking any of this lightly and I only want the best for Ben." I finish what feels like a sermon and close my eyes. I'm tired. Exhausted. The ICU doesn't like overnight visitors but when you promise to make a sizable donation, they seem to forget you're in the room. Only, there isn't a place to sleep, and the only option is a chair.

"The best for Ben?" Brenda shakes her head. "The best for Ben was when I was taking care of him. Everything was fine until you showed up and started waving your money around. Ben, Brad, and I were doing just fine. I would've made sure he made all his appointments."

"You couldn't even keep the house clean." I sit up a bit straighter. "You expected me to pay for a cleaning service because you felt it wasn't your job. The house was a walking Petrie dish of crap because you and Brad refused to clean up after yourselves. I don't want to hear that you would've taken care of Ben because we both know that isn't true. You didn't even take care of him in high school, you certainly weren't going to take care of him now."

"How dare you!" She stands and steps toward me until my dad stands in between us.

"I think you need to cool off, Brenda," Dad says. "I get that you're worried about Ben. We all are. But arguing with Elle, when all she's done is make sure he's being taken care of, isn't going to make him heal any faster. I assure you, everything that can be done, is being done."

"He should've stayed in California."

Dad nods. "And maybe that's true, but we're in Beaumont now and this is where Ben wants to be. Now, I suggest you go in and see your son or sit down. Regardless, you're done speaking to my daughter this way. Ben loves her and it's about time you respect his feelings."

Brenda leans to the side and looks at me. I expect her to sit down but she reaches for her suitcase and walks down the hall. I don't know where she's going or where she's staying, and part of me doesn't care. When Ben wakes up, I'll tell him she's here or was here and he can decide if she wants to see him.

Dad sits back down and reaches for my hand. "She's incredibly jealous of you."

"I don't understand why."

"Because you have money and are able to provide Ben with a lifestyle and family. Two things she couldn't ever give him. She knows, deep down, he'll choose you over her every single time whether he's in your life or not."

"I don't know about that."

Dad chuckles. "Elle, that man loves you. Whether you end up together or not. He's never going to love another woman the way he loves you. In fact, I feel sorry for anyone who comes along if you two aren't together. The next woman, if there is one, will have to compete with the ghost of you, and that's wholly unfair to her."

"You're silly and just trying to make me feel better."

"No, I'm telling you the truth. He looks at you the same way I look at your mother. There's no one else in this world for me, but her. I'm willing to bet Ben feels the same way."

"Thank you for always standing up for me and knowing just the right words to say." I lean into my dad and give him a hug. He squeezes me back, showing me how much he loves me. "As if I'd let anyone talk down to you. You definitely don't deserve the way she treats you."

"Yeah, I know. Still, I appreciate it. I'm going to go check on him. If she comes back, shoot me a text. I don't want you to be alone with her. I don't trust her."

Dad laughs again. "I can take care of myself." I raise my eyebrow at him, and he shakes his head. "Fine, I'll text you."

After another hug, I head back to the ICU. I stand in this doorway and look at Ben's sleeping form. The thought has crossed my mind to start poking and prodding at him to get him to wake up, but I know his body needs the time to heal. I sit down next to Ben and sigh.

"You sigh a lot," his groggily, scratchy voice says.

I jump out of my seat and get right up close to him. "Are you awake?"

He nods slowly.

"Oh, Ben! Oh, God I'm so happy you're awake."

"Me too," he says with a smile. "Dog? What happened?"

I roll my eyes. "Of course, you'd ask about the dog."

He smiles again.

## 26

### BEN

The last thing I remember is playing with a puppy and telling the store clerk I wanted to buy him. Now, though, as I look around, I know I'm not in the pet store anymore, or at home, but in the hospital and I don't have a clue as to how I ended up here. What I do know is that Elle's by my side, right where she said she would be. I reach for her hand, and she gives it to me freely, but not before kissing the back of mine.

"I was so scared," she says with tears streaming down her face. I want to brush them away, but my body is stiff. I ache and my brain is fuzzy, except for images of her and I sitting side by side in white rocking chairs and looking off into the sunset. It's nothing we've ever done, even sitting at her parents or on our balcony, and the dog I remember holding isn't in the picture. But I hear voices. They sound young, and there's a lot of laughter.

"Where am I?" I ask as I move my head from side to side, trying to see my surroundings. Behind me, there's a large window, but there isn't any sunlight coming through.

Is it raining? Evening? I hate the fog in my brain right now. I feel lost and hopeless.

"Beaumont General," Elle says. She brushes her hand across the blanket covering me. "You collapsed at the pet store and an ambulance brought you here."

"Really?"

She nods. "You had a fever, Ben. A bad fever and you're very sick."

"Yeah, the chemo does that."

Elle's lips morph into a fine line and she shakes her head. She inhales deeply and I know she's about to deliver the worst news of my life. "You had a cut on your leg, and it became infected. After tracing our days last week, I figured it happened at the lake when you thought you were bitten by a fish. Quinn went out there and found some rusty nails sticking out of the wood and into the water. We never saw you bleeding because your leg was in the water. You developed sepsis. The doctor believes you're going to make a full recovery, but it's going to take some time, especially with your compromised immune system."

"I'm going to die, aren't I?"

Elle doesn't answer me right off. I look at the ceiling, unable to look into her eyes. "We just have to be more aware of what we're doing. I should've never suggested we go to the lake with everyone or gone back to work. Had we been home, I would've seen the signs. I would've known you had a fever."

I turn my head sharply toward her, which is a mistake. Pain radiates down my side and my stomach rolls. I close my eyes again and practice my breathing exercises until the nausea subsides.

"I don't want you to live like a hermit or give up what you want to do because I might get sick. This is why I didn't tell you, Elle. You shouldn't have to put your life on hold because I have cancer and now this whatever the hell it's called." I let go of her hand and cross my arms over my chest. I'm close to telling her to leave, but I know she won't. She's defiant sometimes. Well, most of the time. She's undoubtedly the most stubborn woman I know.

"Ben, it's not your fault you got another infection or even the first infection. When we were at the lake, neither of us gave it a second thought when you said you got bit by a fish. Let's be honest, what fish is actually going to bite someone?"

"A shark," I say, sarcastically.

"In a lake?" she retorts. "It's not like we were hanging out on the Hudson River and a shark decided to take a stroll up the river."

I shrug.

"Stop being petulant," she tells me. "Shit happens. We deal with it and move on but having a crap attitude or telling me you're going to do this alone isn't going to help. I'm not going anywhere, Ben. And if I want to feel guilty about things, I'm going to."

"But I don't want you to," I say quietly. "I don't want you to feel guilty for staying with me when I'm a walking talking time bomb."

Elle stands abruptly and leans toward me with her finger poised in the air. "Benjamin Miller, I will not tolerate the negativity. You're going to beat this. All of this. The cancer, the sepsis, and whatever else pops the hell up. We're going to fight. Together."

I shake my head and will the tears forming in my eyes to go away. "I've been at this fight for weeks, Elle, and hospitalized twice. It's hard to remain positive."

"We knew the risks," she says, sitting back down. "We

knew infections could happen, and this last one could've been avoided. We just have to be diligent. But I need you to get it through your head, I'm not going anywhere."

Finally, I let the tears flow. "I don't know what I'd do without you." My voice is barely above a whisper, but she hears me. Elle rests her head on my shoulder and her tears soak through my gown, the cotton excuse for pajamas the hospital dresses you in. I put my hand over the top of hers and before I know it, she's crawling into bed, next to me.

"I love you so much, Ben."

"I love you," I tell her and then let out a little laugh. "I had a dream while I was sleeping."

"You were in a coma."

I try to shrug, but my shoulders don't move much. "I think it was before I woke up fully. It was right before I opened my eyes."

"What did you dream about?" she asks. I like that she didn't discount me a second time and believes me when I tell her I had a dream.

"Us, although it was weird. We were there, and I talked about our wedding. You wanted me to tell you about it or something, and then we sat on a porch together. I think we were watching our kids play, which is silly because I can't have kids."

"You froze your sperm, remember."

I grimace at the thought. "It won't be the same."

Elle hugs me tighter. "It will be the same. Whoever you marry will carry your child normally. Inception can still happen like it normally would, it's just different because the doctor has to insert the sperm during ovulation."

"So clinical."

"Eh, just look at it as having all the birth control free sex you want. Most women will be grateful, and you'll definitely save on condoms. Your wife will thank you someday."

"Will she?" I ask.

Elle nods. "If not, then she doesn't grasp what a gift you are to her."

I clear my throat and say her name quietly.

"Huh?" she responds.

"Look at me."

She lifts her head, and our eyes meet. "Will you marry me?"

"What?" her voice cracks.

"Will you allow me to take back everything I said in December and marry me? Forget all the stupid shit I said and did, and consider being my wife? I can't, for the life of me, see myself traversing this path I'm on without you. Not now and not in five, ten or fifteen years. Hell, not ever. When I close my eyes, it's you I see next to me, whether we're at home, in the office or on the road. I realize now, you don't have to give up your career to be my wife or for us to have a family because I can go with you. Your mom took you, Peyton, and Quinn on the road, and we can do the same thing. I know the road isn't the best place to raise a family, but when they're little, who cares, right?"

I adjust and try to sit up a bit, but the strain on my port hurts. I wince and Elle's there to soothe me. Once the pain subsides, I continue, "I was wrong not to see past the importance of having your dad walk you down the aisle. I didn't get it until he shared his thoughts with me, and I was wrong for the things I said to you. I'm sorry, Elle. I'm sorry for making you think I don't care about your job because I do. I see the good you do for young artists and they're lucky to have you. And I'm sorry for not accepting your feelings on planning our wedding. I was angry and being an ass. Instead of fighting for us, I gave up, but you didn't. If I were you, I would've run far and fast, but you didn't because you believe in us."

"I do," she says, nodding.

My hands cup her cheeks and I wipe away her tears. "I'm so damn sorry, Elle, for all the hurt I've caused you. I want to be your husband and the father to your children. I don't even care if we have to wait or you want to do it right now, in this room, just please tell me you'll marry me."

Elle lets out a sob and covers her mouth. She nods frantically while saying, "Yes," through her cries. "Absolutely, yes."

I pull her in for a kiss only for a knock on the door to interrupt us. "Are you freaking kidding me?"

Elle pulls away and laughs. "I'm not supposed to be on your bed," she says quietly and slips back into the chair. I refuse to let go of her hand and keep our fingers locked together tightly.

"Come in."

A doctor and nurse come in, and Elle tells me they've been looking after me since I was brought in. She tells me she's going to be right back and leaves the room. The doctor goes through my illness, and how he wants me to stay in the hospital for my next round of chemo and my off week. He wants to monitor my organs for a bit longer and feels that staying in the hospital is the best solution. For obvious reasons, I don't like the idea, but since I almost killed myself with an imaginary fish bite, I give in. Unfortunately, he also wants me to stay in the ICU to prevent any cross contamination on the other floors and says my risk of future infections is lower while in here. This means, visitation is limited to visiting hours only.

The nurse steps back from the doctor, cracks a smile and winks. I'm assuming something's up. I have a feeling Elle's pitched a fit about visiting hours, and if she hasn't, I bet she might now. When the doctor is done speaking, the nurse asks if I'm up to trying some solid foods and I agree. Honestly, I'm sort of hungry, and was hoping to get out of ICU so Elle could bring me some food. I'm going to have to ask her if she can at least sneak me a cinnamon roll from Whimsicality or something.

When they finally leave, the quiet gives me a moment to reflect and to close my eyes. I'm tired, but I don't want Elle to think I don't want her in here. I do. I need to feel her presence. I don't know where the courage to spill my guts to Elle came from but I'm glad that whatever dream or vision I had made me realize how much of a fool I've been. There's no reason why we can't be happy as a couple, married and with children, while she has a career. I can be the guy that follows his wife on tour, the stay-at-home dad, the cub or girl scout leader. I can do whatever I expected her to do. I should've never expected her to give up her career. It's what she's wanted to do for as long as I've known her. My job is only because of her. I had to find something I thought would keep us together, when I just needed to focus on how we feel about each other.

There's a soft knock on the door and then it opens. Elle enters with Quinn right behind her. Now, I know this is against the rules. One visitor at a time—I remember that much from when Peyton was in ICU.

"Hey, man, it's good to see you." Quinn and I bump fists. "I'm a little confused though. Are we breaking rules now?"

"Elle's broken all the rules since you were admitted,"

Quinn says. He then looks at his sister and I know they're up to something.

Elle gives me a kiss and then holds my hand. "Do you want to get married today?"

"What?" I look from her to Quinn. "I'm not out of here for a couple of weeks, at least." Which doesn't really answer her question about today.

"I know," she says. "But you said something earlier, and it got me thinking. Life is unpredictable. The curve balls that have been thrown our way, we're doing a good job dodging them now, but . . ." She pauses and shakes her head. "I want to dodge them with you, Ben. I don't want to have to wait for someone to look at your chart to prove I'm your person, if that makes sense. If you hadn't signed the directive in Los Angeles, I wouldn't have been able to authorize care for you or be able to see you. I don't like knowing I can't take care of you or that I would've had to depend on your mom to make your medical decisions."

"I wouldn't have liked that either," I interrupt her.

"That makes a whole family of us," Quinn says. "By the way, she's out in the waiting room and is eager to see you, and none too happy that I'm in here before her."

"I can imagine." I'm surprised she's here, to be honest. She wasn't too happy with me when I kicked her out of our house in Malibu.

"Guys, stop interrupting me," Elle demands. I focus on her with my undivided attention. "I love you, Ben, and I think we should get married, today."

"What about your dad walking you down the aisle?"

"We'll have a ceremony later, once you're in the clear and feeling up to it. Right now, I don't want to wait any longer to be your wife."

"But—"

"No buts." She places her finger over my lips. "I want this. I want to be your wife. I don't want to wait."

Deep down, I know she doesn't want to wait because of the cancer. I should tell her no and give her the wedding she wants, the one she deserves, but selfishly I want to be her husband, whether I live past tonight or not.

"Yes, a but," I tell her. "You and your dad have made a compelling case for a wedding because you both want to walk down the aisle. I get it. It makes sense to me now. I don't want you to do something you don't want to do."

Elle cups my cheek. "I want to marry you, Ben. Right here. Right now. My parents will understand, and when you have the all clear, we'll have that massive wedding, in the vineyard, and my dad will walk me down the aisle. We'll party until sunrise and then jet off to the honeymoon of our dreams. I want this for us, but if you want to wait, I understand."

A smile spreads across my face. "Okay. We should see if I can get out of here for a bit. Maybe go to the chapel. There's a chapel here, right?"

Elle nods. "There is, but the chaplain won't marry us."

"Oh, right. No license."

"Right, but there's this website and we fill out the form online, submit our driver's licenses, and they do the rest of the work. There isn't a waiting period."

"But with no one to marry us—"

"That's where I come in," Quinn interrupts. "This website also ordains people and you're looking at the newly minted Quinn James . . ." he pauses and looks at Elle. "Do I have a title?"

She shakes her head slowly. "I don't think so."

"Damn, a title would've been cool. Nonetheless, I can marry you. I mean—"

"We know what you mean, Quinn," Elle says.

She looks at me and smiles. "Or we can wait."

I bring her hand up to my lips and kiss the ring I put on there a while ago. "I don't want to wait."

"Me neither," she says before leaning forward and kissing me.

# 27

## ELLE

It's been eleven days since Ben and I exchanged vows in his ICU room. At first, we weren't going to tell anyone, but asking Quinn to keep something as monumental as us getting married a secret was unfair to him. All I could see playing out was Quinn acting like Joey in FRIENDS with the whole, they don't know we know crap and while it would've been funny, it wasn't right. I thought my parents were going to be hurt, mostly my dad, but surprisingly he accepted that Ben and I had to do it our way—not that this was the way we ever intended to get married—but my dad saw the magnitude of the moment. Life is short. Ben's illness showed us this. I could find every excuse in the world, meaningful or not, to not set a date. Life gave us a reason why to get married.

I pull into my grandpa's driveway and shut the car off. Ben's quiet and looking out the window. I reach for his hand, and he squeezes mine.

"Mack's inside with the puppy."

"Do you think we choose the right name?"

I nod. "I think it's perfect. Come on, he's waiting for you."

"He doesn't even know me."

"He'll know you," I say as I open my door.

Ben and I meet at the front of the car and walk in together. He's nervous about coming home for some reason and I can't figure it out. It's not like he doesn't know my grandfather or Mack, and I made sure everyone went home to give Ben some space. While we love our family, they can be overbearing at times. When we get to the first step, I look at him. "Are you ready?"

He nods.

Ben takes each step slowly, as if he's out of energy. I grow concerned and make a mental note to ask the doctor about a supplement for some energy. When we get to the top of the stairs, I put my hand on his forehead. "Are you feeling okay?" I feel dumb for asking because I know they wouldn't have been discharged if he had a fever.

"Yeah, just afraid."

"Everything will be fine. This was just a minor setback. We'll be more diligent moving forward." After spending as much time as Ben has in the hospital, I learned that some of my excessive cleaning requirements might have been counterproductive for Ben. It seems some bacteria is good for healing, and was reminded that while the ICU is sterile, the walls and floor in Ben's room wasn't being cleaned every day. I've since relaxed, a little bit. We still have a housekeeper, but they're not required to sterilize every single day.

He doesn't say anything as we go into the house. It's quiet. Too quiet. I expect to hear my grandpa moving about or at least the puppy barking. But there's nothing. I start to head into the kitchen, but Ben grabs me around my waist and pulls me to him. He cups my face and leans in for a kiss.

It's the most energetic thing he's done since we left the hospital.

"I love you," he says.

"What did you do?"

"Why do you think I've done something?" he asks, with barely a straight face.

"Benjamin!"

"I'm afraid."

"Of what?"

"Your reaction."

"What are you talking about?"

Ben spins me so my back is facing him. He covers my eyes with his hands and tells me to walk.

"I don't like this, Ben."

"I know, but I have a surprise for you."

I try to remember the layout of the kitchen—the place I grew up in—and I can't. My heart starts beating fast and even though Ben is behind me, I'm nervous. I hear the faint sound of the sliding glass door open, and Ben instructs me to take a step.

I do.

He whispers that he loves me in my ear and then removes his hands from my eyes. Instantly a loud chorus of "Surprise" rings out. My eyes adjust and take in my surroundings. My family, mine and Ben's friends from high school, and all the members of my bands are in the back-yard. There are flowers, balloons, and a three-tiered wedding cake. But it's the banner that catches my eyes the most, "Congratulations, Ben & Elle."

I turn to Ben. "Did you do this?"

"Yeah, I arranged everything with your mom and Peyton. You gave up your dream wedding for me. This is the least I could do."

I pull him into my arms. "But I thought we were going to have a ceremony later."

"Oh, we are. There is nothing in the rule books that say we can't party multiple times. Besides, name one celebrity in the past ten years who hasn't had at least two ceremonies and multiple receptions."

He's right.

"Thank you," I say as I kiss him. Everyone around us hoots and hollers, and someone yells for us to get a room. Believe me, I'd like to. There's nothing like consummating a marriage on a hospital bed in the ICU. I will be forever grateful for the nurses who turned a blind eye to mine and Ben's dalliances.

We thank our family first before greeting our old classmates. Most of these people I haven't seen since we graduated, but some I've run into since our return to Beaumont. I thought it would be odd to catch up with them, but it's been really nice.

Mack yells our names and we both turn to find him and the puppy coming toward us. Ben scoops the puppy up and nuzzles him. This was probably the one rule we didn't break at the hospital—no pets. As much as I wanted to sneak him in, there are so many germs, I didn't want to risk it.

I stand next to my husband as he shows everyone his puppy. "Everyone, I'd like for you to meet Beau."

Everyone aah's at his name, which is the most fitting name for us. Beaumont is where we met, where our lives truly started, and it will always be our home. Right now, it's where we are staying until Ben's better. Sure, we'll go back to Los Angeles and to Malibu, but for now, this is home. Beau represents our life here and us becoming a family. I never thought I'd be a dog mom, but I love it. On the days when I would go work in the studio, Beau came with me. Mack has been picking him up after school and has been training him.

I snuggle into Beau's fur and sigh. When I glance at Ben, he's beaming. While he tried to make today about me or us, it's really about him. I'm confident he's on the path to healing and these bumps in the road are just that—bumps—and proof that we can handle anything thrown our way.

Mack comes back and takes Beau's leash. He parades him around to all the guests while Ben and I do the social thing. When we come around to my parents, I reach for Oliver and inhale his baby scent.

"Any word on the adoption?" I ask.

"We'll know more after Christmas," Dad says.

"Christmas is going to be so much fun. Isn't it Oliver," I say to him.

"Has anyone come forward with a paternity claim?" Ben asks.

"No, not yet." My mom combs Oliver's blond hair with her fingers. "I'm both thankful and saddened. We want to adopt him and make him officially ours, but when I look at him, I think about everything his parents are missing. He's such an amazing little boy."

Oliver says, "Down." I do as he requests, and he toddles over to my dad . . . well, I guess our dad, and holds his arms up so dad will pick him up. A small pang of jealousy goes through as I watch them interact. I don't know why, it's not like I would've remembered being this age with my dad, and the memories I do have are the best. Like the time he let us add color to his tattoos or taught us how to play instruments. While Peyton can play the drums, my musical abilities lie in a somewhat decent singing voice and finding talent that I can turn into stars. I guess you could say I'm the odd man out, but I don't see it like that. We each bring something special to the table in this family.

Peyton and Noah join us, as well as Ben's mom and brother. There's still some animosity there, and I think it will always be there. It's like Brenda resents Ben for befriending me or maybe it's me she resents because I showed Ben a different life. Still, I'm glad they're here for Ben's sake.

"It's time to cut the cake," Mom says and then repeats herself for everyone else. People gather on the deck and Mom guides us on how to cut the cake.

"Are you going to stuff it in my face?" I ask Ben.

He nods. "Without a doubt."

"Rude."

Ben shrugs. "When we do this again next year, I won't. This will be our practice run."

Okay, I can't fault that logic.

We hold the knife, pose for a picture or a million, and then slowly cut a slice out of the cake. Mom is there to help us get it onto the plate and cuts two smaller pieces.

Ben and I each pick up a piece and hold it in the air. "On three," he says.

"One . . . two . . ."

Only Ben doesn't wait until we say three and smashes the cake into my face. I return the favor and then grab the remainder of the piece we cut and smear it all over his face as well.

"That's cheating," he mumbles as cake falls from his face.

"All's fair in love and war."

"Is that so?" Ben pulls me to him and rubs his frosted caked face all over mine. Everyone around us laughs as if this is the funniest thing they've ever seen. When our childish antics are done, I glance at my mom who is not impressed . . . at all.

"Shit," I mumble. I reach for a napkin, hand one to Ben, and start cleaning my face. My mom steps forward with her hands on her hips.

"I wanted one photo, Benjamin. Just one before you two decided to wear the cake. I don't even have a wedding photo of you two so this was my moment." She covers her face with her hands. I have a feeling she's crying.

"Mom." I pull on her wrist so she can see me. "Ben and I are having a full blown ceremony next year."

"You are?"

"Of course," I tell her and then look at my dad. "There's no way I'm skipping all the drama that comes with planning a wedding. Me being a bridezilla, hello! Sign me up."

"Are you mocking me, Elle?" Mom asks.

I think about hugging her, but she'd probably kick my ass. "Not at all. Next year, in a vineyard, Dad will walk me down the aisle, and you'll get all the pretty picture's you want. Oliver will be our ring bearer or maybe he'll walk Beau. It doesn't matter. What does is, Ben and I want a wedding, with all the pomp and circumstance that comes with it."

"Well except the bachelor party," Ben says.

"That's what you think," Quinn hollers from the side.

I put my arm around Ben's waist and lean in. "We took a shortcut because it was right for us, but we still want it all. The flowers, the music, the kiss at sunset," I say as I look at my husband.

"Oh, I'm so happy." Mom doesn't hesitate to hug us. I do my damnedest to keep cake away from her face and hair, but she ends up with some on it.

HEIDI MCLAUGHLIN

The three of us are in this circle until we hear Dad yell, "Oliver, no."

Out of the corner of my eye, I see a chubby little hand digging into the cake and that cake filled hand going right for his mouth. When he hears his name, he turns and giggles, with cake smeared everywhere.

# EPILOGUE

*A*s soon as Ben and I walk into Peyton and Noah's California home, the smell of roasting turkey dominates the ever-present scent of sea salt air. My stomach growls loudly and a bit embarrassingly. Ben laughs, lets Beau off his leash, and drapes his free arm over my shoulders. In his other hand are thank you presents he bought for my family. Well, our family. I told him he didn't have to do anything, but he wanted to make sure everyone knew how much he appreciated the support this year.

We walk into the kitchen and find my mom hovering over the stove with Josie and Jenna. My sister, Eden, Paige, and Nola are off to the side entertaining a very chatty Oliver, and the men in my life are in the other room, watching football. You'd think Noah would rather watch something else, but he still enjoys the game.

"Well, it smells good in here."

My mom is the first to turn and squeal in surprise. It doesn't matter that she saw us last weekend, she's happy to see us all the time.

"I'm starving," I say as I give my mom a hug.

"Good because I made enough to feed an army," she says. "How are you, Ben?" Every day, she asks him how he's doing, and thankfully the answer is always the same.

"Feeling awesome."

I look at him and beam. This year has been rough, to say the least. The difficulties are moments I cherish but also want to forget. I keep them in the back of mind as a reminder of what we've overcome and how we got there to begin with. They're flashes in my life—our life together as a couple—that help us grow, and not something we dwell on. We're coming up on the year anniversary when things started going downhill for Ben and me. It's not a day I want to remember, but it's one we talk about often. We both made mistakes and it took a life-altering situation for us to see the error of our ways. Thankfully, we did.

"What can I do to help?" I ask the moms.

Jenna waves me off. "Don't be silly, go hang with your sister."

"But I want to help," I tell them. I don't really, but it's nice to put the offer out there.

"Someday, all of this will be yours," Josie says. "And the three of us will be sitting on the balcony, with a glass of wine . . ."

"Or the whole bottle," my mom interjects.

"And our children will be in charge of making our feast," Josie laments with a sigh.

I hold in my laughter until I see Jenna bend over and crack up. These ladies are too much and by the looks of it, are already in deep with their wine drinking.

"Oh, I know how you can help," my mom says.

"How?"

"Go plan your wedding. I want to start finalizing everything after the first of the year."

I roll my eyes and Ben laughs. Marrying him in his hospital room was the smartest thing I've done since I told him I loved him years ago. Telling my parents, we got married without them—not so much. At first, they were hurt, which was reasonable, but they understood why we did what we did. However, the "let's set a date" topic popped up as soon as Ben and I told them we were still having a wedding and we've been in planning mode ever since. Ben and I decided on a summer wedding, next year, during a break in the tour. The moms—Katelyn, Josie, and Jenna—are all hands-on deck when it comes to planning. We even consult Brenda on a few of the finer details.

"I'm going to go hang in the other room," Ben says, laughing. He wants no part of the wedding talk. He bends slightly to kiss me, much to the delight of the women in the room. PDA never used to be our thing, and while we still control ourselves, we're a little more open around our family. When we're at work, we keep things strictly professional, unless our office doors are closed. I watch him and Beau disappear around the corner.

I make my way to where my sister and the others are. When Oliver sees me, he lights up and waddles his way toward me. He's walking now and a holy terror. When mom or dad need a break, they don't ask us to watch him, they ask us if we can wrangle him for a bit because that's what it's like when he's around. The boy can Houdini himself out of his play yard and likes to climb on everything. Betty Paige jokes that Oliver is going to be the first one in our family to climb Mt. Everest. Something tells me she's right.

"Dog," he says.

"With Uncle Ben," I tell him. "Go find Daddy." I point to the other room and Oliver takes off like he's being chased.

As of late, I've seen more of Paige than I have of my

sister. Ben and I keep two residences, our house in Malibu and one in Beaumont. The music scene is really taking off there, and Liam is in the process of buying Ralph's. Ralph, the longtime owner, doesn't have any kids and wants to retire. Funnily enough, Liam wants to own a bar. Honestly, I think Liam wants to own the entire town and if given the chance, he will. No one can say he isn't giving back to the community that supported him when he was a teenager. He's done so much in the revitalization of Beaumont, it's crazy. A few of the town council members want him to run for Mayor, but Liam says politics are not in his future. He's happy doing what he's doing and likes the flexibility his life affords him. In February, once football season is over, 4225 West is going on tour, with both Plum and Sinful Distraction as their opening acts. It's nice when a manager like me has some connections. This tour will catapult Plum to the next level. They're on the cusp of being something amazing.

"How's surfing?" I ask Eden.

"It's good," she says. "I'm heading to Hawaii next week to get ready for a competition and then to Costa Rica."

"That's incredible. Your videos are spectacular."

"Thanks." She smiles brightly.

"What do you do about school?" Peyton asks.

"I have a tutor; she comes with us," Eden says.

"Are you going on tour with the band?" Paige asks. She looks at Eden with pleading eyes.

Eden nods. "I am. I wouldn't miss it."

I elbow Peyton. "These kids are lucky. Mom rarely let us go on tour at their age."

"I know. I'm jealous."

"Wait, you're going too, right?" Paige asks us.

"I'll come to a few, but I have to work," Peyton says.

"I'll be at some stops," Nola says. "The bus life isn't glamorous. I don't know how you do it."

Peyton and I laugh. It's definitely something you get used to, and it's much easier if you grow up with it.

"I'll be there," I tell her. "My bands, remember."

"I can't wait to see Plum. O. M. Geeeeee. I am so excited," Paige says as she claps her hands. She met them when they came to the studio and fell in love with their music. She's asked me a few times to bring them back to Beaumont, but they haven't had the time. I half expected her to show up at the studio when she arrived in Los Angeles the other day, but Liam came alone. I think this is the first time his daughter is obsessed with a band and he's not sure how to handle her fangirling moments.

The moms yell for dinner and we all gather in Peyton and Noah's massive dining room. This is the first time they're hosting, and it's only because Noah isn't playing this weekend. Normally, we're either in Portland or we're celebrating without them. I hate that we're all so spread out and I don't think it would be so bad if Noah's job wasn't during the heart of the holidays. Peyton missed Oliver's first Halloween a few weeks ago. Mom and Dad dressed him up as a teddy bear and he was the cutest thing ever. Ben and I had a blast walking around the neighborhood with him, but it was seeing my parents with him that sealed the deal. Ben and I are ready to start trying for a family.

We all sit down, and I rest my hand on Ben's leg. Having been through what he has, you learn not to take any moment for granted. We're more in tune with each other and we talk about everything. The littlest things like whether we should change the brand of toilet paper we buy, or which gas station is one cent cheaper are something we talk about instead of one of us making a household decision.

We realized even this kind of communication makes our relationship stronger.

Everyone starts passing bowls of potatoes, vegetables, salad, and everything else the moms made around the table. I take a little of everything because I know I'll want seconds, and then I'll have thirds in a few hours. There's something about reheated Thanksgiving dinner that's better than the actual dinner itself. Not everyone will agree with me and that's okay. I have my vices, and this is one of them.

Once everyone has filled their plates, we go around and say one thing we're thankful for. I've thought about what I'm going to say for a couple of months now, wavering back and forth between a few things. There are so many moments and people in my life, that it's hard to pinpoint one action or event that stands out, but I think I found it.

When it's my turn, I clear my throat. I know everyone expects me to be thankful for Ben, and I am. He knows this. I tell him every day. Each morning when I see his eyes, I remind him that I'm incredibly lucky to have him next to me, to be able to call him my husband, and to hear him tell me that he loves me.

"I'm thankful for my brother, Quinn." I look across the table at him and he dips his head. "Without you, I'm not sure Ben would be my husband today. You never gave up on your friendship with him and you knew exactly how to push me back to him. You love without reservation. I'm thankful for each and every day I get to call you my brother."

I raise my glass to him, but he stares at me. He pushes his chair back and walks around the table. I stand and fall into his arms when he opens them. "I love you, Elle," he whispers to me.

"I love you too, Quinny."

When I sit back down, I glance at our dad and catch him wiping his cheeks. I hope he knows how much he means to me, that without him I wouldn't be half the person I am today. Ben leans over and kisses my cheek. "That was beautiful," he says.

He clears his throat and looks around the table. "There are a couple of things I'm thankful for, so if you'll bear with me for a moment."

Everyone laughs and Jimmy says, "I think you've earned your time, mate."

"I appreciate it." Ben stands, which surprises me. "I'm thankful for my beautiful wife, who loves me despite my lack of . . ."

"Benjamin." The tone of my voice warns him not to finish the sentence regardless of Jimmy egging him on.

Ben laughs. "I'm thankful for my beautiful wife, the life we live, for Beau, and for this family who took me in as their own. I would not be here today, if it wasn't for your love and support. With that said, I'm also thankful for my doctors, and the radiologist who read my recent scans. As of right now, the cancer hasn't returned."

Everyone claps. We've had this news for a couple of days, but he wanted to wait until today to share it with everyone. Ben looks at me and then back at everyone. "I'm not out of the woods yet, but this is the first step, and it's a good one." He raises his glass, and everyone says, "Here, here."

We finish dinner and clean-up, and we're about to head outside when the doorbell chimes. I'm closest to the door and open it. "Hello," I say to the young man on the other side. "Can I help you?"

"Yes, I'm Rush Fennimore. I'm here to see Eden Davis if she's available?"

*Ooh!*

"Eden," I yell her name. "There's a young man here to see you."

She comes around the corner, clad in a bikini top with her wet suit covering her legs. Her eyes widen in surprise and then she sprints to the door. Within seconds her arms are around Rush and they're kissing.

"What are you doing here? I didn't think I'd see you until tomorrow."

"I came a day early to surprise you."

Eden squeals and kisses him again.

"I can hear you," Jimmy yells from the other room and I start to laugh.

"Eden, why don't you invite your friend in."

"Yes, come in. You have to meet everyone," she says, dragging the poor kid by his hand. He smiles as he walks by, and I can see why Eden is smitten with him.

"Hey, Rush," Quinn says. They shake hands and I look at my brother oddly. He shrugs and mouths that he'll tell me later. I swear he's the secret keeper.

"Everyone, I'd like for you to meet Rush," Eden says. "Rush, this is . . . well, literally everyone in my family." Rush goes to everyone and shakes their hands. While this happens, Quinn tells me Eden and Rush met last Christmas in Vermont and have been traveling to see each other every few months. Rush is an Olympic hopeful in snowboarding, which Quinn believes is why Jimmy is so chill about Eden having a boyfriend.

Peyton asks if I want to go outside with the teens, and I agree. Eden shows Rush where to change into a wetsuit and we all gather at the shoreline to watch her do her thing. When I see Betty Paige and Mack walk off, I bump Peyton's arm.

"Are they having sex?"

She shrugs. "Noah's talked to Mack and he assures Noah they're not doing anything they shouldn't be doing. I don't think Mack would jeopardize the living arrangement."

"I can't believe Nick isn't back yet."

"I know, it's been almost a year. Mack seems okay though. He spent most of his summer with Noah between Portland and Beaumont, and he's thriving with Liam and Josie. Liam hasn't missed a game of his since Mack moved in."

"I figured Mack would've gone to live with you and Noah before Liam."

"Same. We would've taken him for sure."

Peyton and I watch the two love birds until they're out of sight. "They're cute," I say nodding toward Eden and Rush.

"They're so opposite. She's summer and he's winter. It's fun to see."

I bump my shoulder with hers. "My gut tells me something's wrong, but I can't pinpoint what. You and Noah look incredibly happy, sometimes too happy," I tell her. "So, what gives? Where's my bright and cheery twin? What's bothering you?" I ask her. "You seem down."

Peyton leans into me and rests her head on my shoulders. "Life's . . . I don't know," she says. She lifts her head and looks at me. "Noah and I are desperately trying to get pregnant. We've done everything we can, but the doctors think there's too much damage to my pelvis. I have a lot of scarring from the accident."

I reach for her hand and hold it tightly.

"I've miscarried twice."

"Peyton," I gasp.

"I haven't told anyone because I feel like a failure as a

woman. I barely found out I was pregnant and then I wasn't."

"Honey, I'm so sorry." I pull her into my arms. "Oh, sweetie."

"I'm okay," she tells me, but I don't know that she is. "I have something to ask you."

"Of course, anything."

She looks at me with her tear streaked eyes and tries to smile. "Will you carry a baby for me?"

My mouth drops open and my heart falls to my stomach. I would do anything to help my sister and her husband have a baby. "I can't," I say quietly.

"Can't or won't?" she asks as her face falls.

"I can't, Peyton. Ben and I are . . ." I pause, knowing I'm about to break the pact I made with Ben. I clear my throat. "We're starting IVF. We want to start a family."

Realization hits her and she smiles. "I understand. The timing . . ."

"If Ben . . ."

"I get it, Elle. If I had asked last year—"

"I would've said yes in a heartbeat."

"I know," she says quietly. I pull her to me, and we hug for a long time. I cry for the babies she's lost and the pain she's going through. She's been through so much. I hate that her heart is broken. When we part, I brush her hair away from her wet cheeks.

"So, what's next?" I ask her.

Peyton shrugs. "There's this surgery. They go in and scrape away the scar tissue or something. I don't know. I wasn't paying attention because I'm angry . . . at myself, the truck that hit Kyle's car and the damage it did to my body, and for losing those babies. Noah paid attention though. He's my rock. He has the entire procedure memorized and then IVF. The specialist says I might need a couple rounds. Asking you was an easy way out. Noah and I have talked about surrogacy but it scares me. You're the only one I'd trust."

"Want me to wait?" I ask her, knowing this is something I should discuss with Ben. Deep down, I think he'll be on the same page because he knows how important Peyton is to me. "I think it would be kind of fun to be pregnant together." I know the chances of us getting pregnant at the same time are slim, but it's worth a shot.

She snorts. "Would you do that?" Her eyes light up. "I can schedule the surgery as soon as I get back to Portland."

I nod. "I'll wait. I want our babies to be born at the same time," I tell her. "Mom would love it. Imagine all the party planning she could do. I'll come to you. We'll do this together, all of it. Every step of the way. You hold my hand, I'll hold yours."

Peyton smiles. "I'd like that."

"Me too."

We stay there, sitting with our heads together, watching the surf and I imagine our children playing in the sand, with their extended family surrounding them. When Ben, Beau, and Noah join us, I suggest Ben, Beau, and I go for a walk, and I ask him what he thinks about waiting until after Peyton's surgery.

"I think you're the most amazing, selfless, woman I have ever known. I don't mind waiting if it's going to make you happy. Besides, my swimmers aren't going anywhere anytime soon."

Ben cups my cheeks and kisses me. "I love you, Benjamin Miller."

"I love you too, Elle Miller."

# THE TAYLOR SWIFT PLAYLIST

Enchanted
Back to December
Haunted
State of Grace
Red
All too Well
I Almost Do
The Last Time
Everything has Changed
Ronan
This Love
Better Man

# ALSO BY HEIDI MCLAUGHLIN

## THE BEAUMONT SERIES

Forever My Girl

My Everything

My Unexpected Forever

Finding My Forever

Finding My Way

12 Days of Forever

My Kind of Forever

Forever Our Boys

Forever Mason

The Beaumont Boxed Set - #1

## THE BEAUMONT SERIES: NEXT GENERATION

Holding Onto Forever

My Unexpected Love

Chasing My Forever

Peyton & Noah

Fighting For Our Forever

Give Me Forever

A Beaumont Family Christmas

## THE PORTLAND PIONEERS:

A BEAUMONT SERIES NEXT GENERATION

SPIN-OFF

Fourth Down

Fair Catch

False Start


CAPE HARBOR SERIES

After All

Until Then


THE ARCHER BROTHERS

Here with Me

Choose Me

Save Me

Here with Us

Choose Us


The Archer Boxset


LOST IN YOU SERIES

Lost in You

Lost in Us


THE BOYS OF SUMMER

Third Base

Home Run

Grand Slam

Hawk

THE REALITY DUET

Blind Reality

Twisted Reality

SOCIETY X

Dark Room

Viewing Room

Play Room

THE CLUTCH SERIES

Roman

STANDALONE NOVELS

Stripped Bare

Blow

Sexcation

HOLIDAY NOVELS

Santa's Secret

It's a Wonderful Holiday

THE DATING SERIES

A Date for Midnight

A Date with an Admirer

A Date for Good Luck

A Date for the Hunt

A Date for the Derby

A Date to Play Fore

A Date with a Foodie

A Date for the Fair

A Date for the Regatta

A Date for the Masquerade

A Date with a Turkey

A Date with an Elf

# ABOUT HEIDI MCLAUGHLIN

Heidi McLaughlin is a New York Times, Wall Street Journal, and USA Today Bestselling author of The Beaumont Series, The Boys of Summer, and The Archers.

In 2012, Heidi turned her passion for reading into a full-fledged literary career, writing over twenty novels, including the acclaimed Forever My Girl.

Heidi's first novel, Forever My Girl, has been adapted into a motion picture with LD Entertainment and Roadside Attractions, starring Alex Roe and Jessica Rothe, and opened in theaters on January 19, 2018.

*Don't miss more books by Heidi McLaughlin! Sign up for her newsletter, join the fun in her fan group, or get text updates. Text GETHEIDISBOOKS to (833) 926-1009!*

*Connect with Heidi!*
www.heidimclaughlin.com

Made in the USA
Middletown, DE
19 August 2023